LOVE'S LEGACY

Natalie Kleinman

SAPERE
BOOKS

LOVE'S LEGACY

Published by Sapere Books.

20 Windermere Drive, Leeds, England, LS17 7UZ,
United Kingdom

saperebooks.com

ISBN: 978-1-80055-647-8

CHAPTER ONE

Patience clutched at her father's arm. "Don't leave me, please Papa," she pleaded. "I can't bear for you to leave me." He had been ill for several months now, and had been coughing painfully for the past three days. The doctor had informed Patience that nothing could be done and she had prayed that her father would improve until the end. But it was too late. The hand she gripped so tightly was as lifeless as the man whose bed she sat beside.

Time lost all meaning as Patience stared out of the window, alone with her thoughts. The sun rose on a bleak winter morning, sending a weak shaft of light which fell upon her father's face.

With the passing of Reverend Nicholas Worthington went also the last vestige of her security. At twenty-two years old Patience was alone, with only a small bequest from her father to support herself. Almost his last words had been to urge her to look in his desk, to take the letter she would find there to his older brother. "You must go to him. He will take care of you," he'd said. But they had been estranged from her uncle for as long as she could remember. How could she look to him for aid?

"I will, Papa. I promise." Patience would have promised him anything in that moment to give him a little comfort as he passed from this world to the next.

Uttering a sigh that came from the depths of her soul, she rose and pulled the sheet over him. She needed to summon the doctor. She also needed a man of the cloth, but that man had been her father. So suddenly had his illness come upon him that no other had yet been appointed in his place. When that happened, her home would be taken from her and she would have to move on. With one last look over her shoulder, she went slowly from the room to search for the letter. Whether or not she would act upon her father's wish was something she had not as yet decided.

Three weeks later, Patience Worthington looked from the carriage back at the house in Oakenchurch where she'd spent her entire life. It stood next to a stone church with a small steeple, and overlooked the village graveyard where her father had been laid to rest beside his wife. On the edge of her seat her companion, Mary Petersham, wept into a handkerchief. Patience tore her eyes away and attempted to comfort her erstwhile governess. When her tenure had come to an end, both the reverend and his daughter had begged her to stay and she, having no other position in place, accepted gratefully. Only ten years separated them, and they had long since abandoned any employer-employee relationship and become firm friends.

"Don't cry, Mary. We will do, you'll see." But her own tears were not far beneath the surface. "And if this uncle of mine spurns me we can set up together somewhere, a small business, maybe," she said in an effort to lighten the tone.

"Doing what, may I ask?" Mary replied with a sniff as she pulled herself together. "Maybe you'd like us to take in washing or suchlike. You're Quality born and not fit nor meant for such menial work."

Patience laughed, glad to see Mary's no-nonsense attitude return. "You are yourself of gentle birth, and yet you undertook to educate me."

"My circumstances left me with no choice but to find employment, as you are aware."

"And it may be that mine will be thus similar. We shall have to see what happens when we reach our destination. But for all the learning you tried to give me, I'm a simple girl at heart. You and Papa did your best to instil some knowledge in me, but even you will admit that my voice is indifferent and my attempts to play the piano would drive any enthusiast from the room."

Mary didn't deny it. It was the truth, after all. "You set a fine stitch, though. And your grasp of French is good, though I flatter myself to say so."

"That then will be the answer if his lordship rejects me. Now that the war is over and Napoleon tucked safely away, we can travel to France and set up as dressmakers. I knew you would find a solution, Mary."

"Don't be daft," she replied, smiling in spite of the circumstances. "What you need is a husband! 'Tis a pity you didn't see fit to take Major Saxby when he offered for you."

"To be sure, Major Saxby is a worthy gentleman. And that was the problem. I have had no adventure in my life, Mary. Worthy is the last thing I want."

Recovering from a fit of the giggles, they continued in silence for a while. To herself the young Miss Worthington had long acknowledged that marriage, that most traditional of all occupations for a young woman, would be the most expedient. Two things, though, stood as a bar to this being a resolution. Firstly, she had to find a man willing to marry her, other than the major of course, and secondly she had no ambition to enter the state of matrimony without love. Patience had always believed that her mother had given up everything for love of her father. Cut off by family upon her marriage, she had told her fourteen-year-old daughter that there was nothing more precious in life than the devotion of a good man. Only death would part her and Nicholas, and it had done just that twelve months later, when pregnancy in her more mature years had taken both her and her unborn babe. The reverend's faith had wavered but returned with renewed vigour as he undertook to raise his daughter alone.

"Why did Mama's people not come to her funeral, Papa?" the young Patience had asked, knowing her father had written to inform them of her passing.

"Bitterness is a self-wounding and destructive sentiment, my child. If they choose not to pay their respects, it is their loss. I shall pray for them."

But her father's hadn't been the only letter she'd found in his desk. Her mother too had left one for her. *To be opened when your Papa and I are both gone*, it had said.

My dearest child,

If you are reading this, it can only mean that Nicholas and I are no longer of this world. There are things I owe it to you to tell, though I lacked the courage while I lived. My excuse to myself was always that you were too young to understand. You will not know that I left my parents' home under a cloud, for I behaved as only a foolish young girl can. I did not love your father when first we married. This will come as a shock to you, I know, but I grew to love him more than life itself. He rescued and made an honest woman of me when my family cut all ties. They had good reason. There has been no contact since then, but you must know that I had two sisters, both older and both married before the scandal that engulfed me occurred. I have followed them over the years and can tell you they are now deceased but that you have one cousin, Clara Buxton, who is married and lives in Bath. Seek her out if you will. She may forgive me

where they could not. If I leave you anything, Patience, it is the boundless love your father and I shared. This is our legacy to you.
  Mama

What could her mother have done that was so bad as to be rejected by her family? Was the opinion of others worth more than their daughter's happiness? Would she, Patience, find kinder treatment from her father's brother? She placed little reliance on it, after so many years without communication of any kind. So much so that she had not even written to her uncle to inform him of her father's demise. It was only later, when weighing up the prospects of an uncertain future, that she made the decision to approach the viscount, no other plan having presented itself to her, and the prospect seemingly more hopeful than any approach to her mother's relations. But she went with an anxiety she could not easily suppress.

The distance from Oakenchurch to Worthington Place on the outskirts of Bath was sufficiently short as to enable Patience and Mary to complete the journey within a single day, even at this time of the year when the days had yet to lengthen. With her worldly possessions piled on the hired carriage, Patience gave no indication to Mary of her inward trepidation until they turned into the long drive. Looming before them in the fast-fading light was a mansion of considerable proportions. It stood three storeys high, though Patience suspected a basement too which she could not see from her current vantage point. At least four times as broad as it was tall, she couldn't imagine its depth. She had never been in such a house before. She reached for Mary's hand with fingers that shook uncontrollably.

"Try not to fret, Patience," the other said, squeezing them reassuringly. "All will be well, you'll see. He can hardly turn you from the door at this time of day. Why, it'll be dark in not too many minutes."

The practicality of Mary's remarks succeeded in settling her nerves a little, but as she mounted steps that were flanked by two large stone pillars, it was all she could do to prevent her trembling knees from striking together. She had to remind herself that once this had been her father's home. Patience raised her hand to the knocker, but before she could employ it the door was opened, causing her to lose balance slightly and stumble forward. A hand caught her elbow and she was escorted into a hallway, Miss Petersham hard upon her heels.

"Forgive me, madam, but I saw your carriage approach. I had no intention of disconcerting you," said the butler in a manner that reassured her sufficiently to enable her to collect her wits, which had for a moment deserted her. "Is the master expecting you?"

"He is not. Perhaps you could tell him that his niece is here, his brother's daughter," she said in a voice that sounded far more confident than she felt. She saw what she construed as a rather startled expression in the man's face before he replied, "Allow me to escort you and your companion into the small sitting room," he said, leading the way. "And what name shall I give?"

"Miss Patience Worthington."

The butler bowed himself from the room and Patience heaved a sigh of relief, removed her muff and pelisse and sat down to wait, urging Mary to do the same. It was close on ten minutes before anyone appeared, and they had ample opportunity to survey their surroundings. The salon was tastefully but expensively furnished in soft shades of green, with pastoral paintings hung on either side of the fireplace. Logs were burning in the hearth, from which the ladies took comfort.

When the door opened once more, it was to herald the entry of a man who was very evidently not her father's older sibling. She judged him to be perhaps five or six years her senior, and he was handsome beyond any man she had ever seen. His dark hair was arranged Brutus fashion and his person was as neat as a pin. But who was he?

"I am sorry to have kept you waiting, Miss Worthington. Sedlescombe tells me you are my niece, but as we can both see that is most definitely not the case. You have perhaps been misinformed," he said, glancing from one lady to the other, uncertain as to whom he should be addressing.

Patience removed any doubts when, in response to his bow, she rose and dropped a short curtsey, her smile reflecting that of her host. Happy at last to have something to get to grips with, even though she didn't know what that something might be, she said in what she hoped was a self-composed manner, "No, that much of course is plain. It may be that we are cousins. The man I have come to see is Lord Lacey."

"I am he."

"But that's impossible! My uncle was some six years senior to my father." And that's when the truth struck her and she raised a hand to her chest, inwardly chastising herself for not having foreseen such a circumstance. She stepped back a pace. "I see I have made a grave error. My parent passed away only recently. It never occurred to me that yours might have done the same."

In the viscount's eyes lurked a smile, but all he said was, "I suggest you sit down, Miss Worthington. And Miss...?" he enquired, turning to Mary.

"Forgive me. Permit me to introduce my friend, Miss Petersham. You must allow me some confusion, which I put forward as an excuse for my bad manners."

"Not at all. Now, why don't I ring for some refreshment, and then perhaps you may tell me what it is you wish me to do for you."

Where to begin? Patience drew a letter from her reticule and handed it to him without a word, sitting again while he made himself familiar with its contents. She herself had no idea what it contained. It had been sealed and was directed to Viscount Lacey of Worthington. He finished reading and folded it just as the promised refreshments were brought in, and conversation was not practical for some moments until the footman withdrew. Patience realised she was exceedingly hungry, having taken nothing since breakfast that morning. Mary, she was certain, would be feeling the same. Still holding the paper in his hand, her cousin — for who else could he be? — took up a lounging position by the fire. She would have preferred him to sit.

"Much is made clear in this letter, but it leaves us in a difficult position to say the very least. Are you familiar with what it says, Miss Worthington?"

"No, for you must know that it was sealed, and my knowledge of it came only when my father was on his deathbed." Naturally anxious to know what it contained, she continued, "Perhaps, if it isn't too much of an imposition to ask, you might make its contents known to me."

The smile returned, replacing the frown which had been causing Patience no little anxiety. "Yours is not the imposition." That didn't sound good. "It would seem your father and mine had a falling out many years ago, for what reason I know not. His letter gives me to understand that your parent was a man of the church, a not unusual occupation for a younger son. Apparently, though he was the incumbent of his parish, no provision was made for his family following his demise. He begs my own father will put aside their differences and take you, Miss Worthington, into his household." The viscount paused, seemingly waiting for a response. Patience didn't know what to say, though her agitation showed in the biting of her lip.

He seemed to notice her uncertainty, for he said, "This is too large a subject and it is far too late into the day to resolve it now. May I ask that you join my mother and me for supper? In the meantime, I will have rooms prepared for you both. I am sure you will wish to retire for a while to adjust to your altered circumstances."

"You are very kind, my lord."

"Kind? As a gentleman I have little choice in the matter."

Despair flooded in until Patience realised he was smiling and that he expected her also to enjoy what little amusement there was in the situation. Being possessed of a lively sense of humour she smiled in return, her pent-up emotions finding some relief in the absurdity of the situation. "We have, my father and I, put you in an invidious position, have we not?"

"I have ever liked a challenge, Miss Worthington. Now, if you will excuse me, I will set things in motion. Am I correct in assuming your carriage to be a hired vehicle?"

She acknowledged that it was.

"Then I shall have your luggage removed and send the driver on his way. Mrs Abberwick will come for you when your rooms are ready. In the meantime, please continue to refresh yourselves. I will go to inform my mother of what has occurred and I look forward to introducing you to her later."

There was a small dressing room between the chamber that had been allocated to Patience and the next one along the corridor, which was to accommodate Mary. It didn't take them long to unpack one or two things, and they quickly changed out of their travelling clothes into something more suitable for the evening. The rest stayed where it was in the trunks, because there was as yet no certainty that they would be remaining at Worthington Place for an extended period. Mrs Abberwick had told them to make themselves comfortable and that the sitting room they'd just vacated was at their disposal. Considering at first that they might remain upstairs for a while, thoughts of the fire lured them back down and they settled themselves to wait until summoned for supper.

"The viscount seems quite charming, don't you think, Patience?"

"Certainly he reacted well to what must after all be an unwelcome situation."

"How so, unwelcome?"

"Would you like strangers arriving on your doorstep so late in the day that courtesy compelled you to invite them to stay? I believe I would not and cannot think why I didn't foresee the inevitability. I am considerably embarrassed. We might easily have lodged nearby and called tomorrow at a more convenient time."

Mary smiled conspiratorially. "Yes, but with nowhere near the comfort afforded us here. Mrs Abberwick spoke of having a fire lit in our bedchambers. Such luxury."

"You are without shame, Mary Petersham!" said Patience, but she too was smiling.

They had not been waiting many minutes when the door opened to admit Lord Lacey, and it was immediately obvious from the gravity of his expression that all was not well.

"I am happy to see you settled and I apologise for disturbing you, but there is something I need to say."

He drew up a chair covered with green brocade and flung himself into it, crossing one long leg over the other before speaking again. Patience could only wonder what was amiss, for the man before her was evidently feeling a degree of discomfort. She said nothing but merely folded her hands in her lap and waited.

"Miss Worthington, Miss Petersham, it would appear that the mystery is in some way to being resolved, though not perhaps in a manner any of us would desire. My mother will not after all be joining us this evening but will take her meal in her private drawing room. It would seem that the source of the estrangement between our families stems not from our paternal parents but from their wives. Mama was several years younger than my father. It was through her that your own mother met the brothers, for they were introduced at a soirée they were all attending. Apparently your mother and mine had been friends forever and as such were seen everywhere together." Lord Lacey unfolded his legs and leaned back in his chair. He seemed to be puzzling as to how to proceed.

Patience, her nerves stretched, could not wait to hear what was to come next. "And?" she said, rather more sharply than she had intended.

He smiled, but it was a little twisted. "And, Miss Worthington, there was a rift which to this day has never been healed. In spite of the attachment between my parents — it seemed the announcement of their betrothal was expected any day — your mother, aware though she was of the situation, threw her cap at him in such a way as to shock their entire acquaintance. There could be no doubt that she hoped to win him for herself. As our grandfather's heir he was considered a great catch, and it seems Miss Longfield would not be turned. Heedless of the figure she was making of herself, her pursuit of him was relentless."

Patience made a move, as if to interrupt, but the viscount held up his hand. "Allow me to finish, if you please, for this is as unpleasant for me to say as it must be for you to hear. From being an acknowledged beauty who might well have had her pick of the beaux of the time, Elizabeth Longfield was shunned by Society. It was only the intervention of my uncle, who it seems was infatuated with her, which saved her from being disgraced entirely. Rejected by her world, she had little other choice than to accept his offer. Your father, who at the time resided still at Worthington Place, immediately sought a living in another parish. My information is that they were married quietly and, until you arrived here today, little was known about what happened to them."

"So that's what she meant," Patience exclaimed, more to herself than the rest, whereupon she jumped to her feet and began pacing up and down.

"Patience, dearest, please calm yourself," said Mary, her own agitation made evident by the tremor in her voice.

"Calm! How can I be calm when such slander is levelled at my poor mother? I have never seen two people so much in love as my parents. I repudiate your claim, sir," she said, turning on the hapless viscount even as she remembered her mother's words and realised the accusation must be true.

Gideon Worthington was not to be intimidated. Without any loss of composure, though there was fire in his eyes, he too rose to face the spitfire before him. "Whatever might have been the relationship between your parents, I am naturally not in a position to comment upon. However, Miss Worthington, I totally resent your implication that my mother is bearing false witness. I ask that you retract your accusation of slander."

Patience took a deep breath and made a visible effort to control herself, not being in the habit of making overly dramatic gestures. However, in the light of the events of the past few weeks and her own perception of her whole life, she said, "I cannot, and as such I see that my position here is untenable. Miss Petersham and I will leave in the morning."

"And do what?" he asked, not attempting to disguise the sarcasm so evident in his pronunciation. "You have sought my protection, and I will not be accused of turning you away. We are no great distance from Bath, and it may be possible that ultimately we can establish you there. But for the time being, I see no alternative than for you to remain here. You will have noticed as you turned into the drive that there is a rather fine gatehouse. It is at present unoccupied. I propose that you take up residence there while we consider what action to take. It is evident you can't stay in this house, but neither can I turn you out onto the streets."

"I do not ask for your charity, sir!"

"But that's exactly what you have done by coming here today, Miss Worthington. Let us, if we can, take the heat out of this conversation. You have nowhere to go and, from what you have confided in me, little means with which to support yourself. It would be wise, I feel, to keep this matter within the family. Your future may depend on it."

"I do not care for such things."

"It seems then that there is much of your mother in you."

"You are insulting, my lord, and I will not be so beholden unto you."

"You asked for it. Now, if you will excuse me, I think it best if we do not after all dine together this evening. A little space might help us each take stock of the situation. I shall have your meal served in here and hope you will join me for breakfast in the morning, after which I will escort you to the gatehouse. I shall in the meantime have it made ready for your occupation." Not waiting for her reply, he left the room without another word.

Patience stamped her foot in frustration and Mary dissolved into tears.

"Don't cry, Mary. The situation is by far too serious for tears." Patience's pacing resumed, then stopped again. "I don't suppose you'd like to reconsider my French dressmaking idea?" she asked, her sense of humour never far beneath the surface. Her friend's look told her all she needed to know. "Very well then, but we have to think carefully about our next move."

"It seems to me our next move has already been planned for us."

"I don't mean the gatehouse. Though I wouldn't admit it to his lordship, the idea appeals far more than staying in this huge edifice, which in any case is out of the question now. Lady Lacey is the last person I want to risk bumping into."

"She could maybe tell you something about your mother as a young woman," Mary said hopefully. Patience had told her nothing of her mother's letter.

"From what her son has told us, I doubt if we'd hear anything that would resemble the Mama I remember."

They were interrupted by the arrival of supper and conversation ceased for a while. It was easy to see that Patience was preoccupied with her thoughts. Whether they were of her father and the life she'd left behind or of her uncertain future could not be determined from her expression, but Mary had enough sense to know when to keep her own counsel. They decided to retire early, it having been a long and stressful day.

"There is nothing more we can do tonight, Mary. It is to be hoped we will see our way more clearly once we're established in the gatehouse, but I cannot and will not remain there indefinitely. It goes beyond all feelings of self-respect to do so."

Proud as she was, Patience had still been able to view the prospect of putting herself into her uncle's care with a certain composure, albeit reluctantly. He was family, after all. But her uncle was no more. The son didn't want her. He was only doing what he saw as his duty. Her aunt refused even to meet her. No, the sooner she could contrive a way to leave, the better.

CHAPTER TWO

Breakfast the next day was a somewhat formal affair, Gideon Worthington polite but distant, informing Patience that all was in train for her removal to the gatehouse at her convenience. Of his mother there was no sign. Patience was docile and just as cold as he. There was, she felt, no point in antagonising him further. Once removed from this place, she was certain she would be able for the most part to avoid him. She certainly didn't anticipate him seeking her out more than was absolutely necessary, and then only to advise her of such arrangements as he deemed fit to put in place in his obviously managing way. Well, she wasn't having any of it, but she was careful to make only fleeting eye contact with him, for she felt sure he would observe the sparks flying from her gaze. Mary was on tenterhooks, knowing that the meek front Patience was portraying was totally out of character. She feared every moment that her friend would betray herself.

Viscount Lacey, his own breakfast finished, made to leave the room, turning towards them as he reached the door. "I hope you will find it convenient to leave in, let us say, two hours," he said, glancing at the clock on the mantelpiece. "I shall have your luggage brought down to the hall. I rode over to the gatehouse earlier this morning and the servants were already hard at work. All should be ready for your occupation by the time we arrive."

"You are too kind, sir."

Gideon took the words at face value. Mary trembled inwardly. This was not the Patience she knew.

"I have allocated some of my staff to see to your needs, and they will remain there while you are in residence. I think that is all. I will see you when it is time to leave."

As he closed the door behind him, Mary blurted out, "My dear, my heart was in my mouth for fear of what you might say. I expected at any moment that you would storm out of the room."

Patience turned the full steel of her grey eyes upon her friend, though her anger was not directed at that unfortunate woman. They softened as she saw the distress she was causing. "It seems everything is arranged and we are left with nothing to do but comply. He's a cold one, isn't he? And oh so polite. Well, I too can be polite. Don't worry. I have myself well under control. It is necessary, is it not, until we find a way out of this mess? But I've had a night in which to consider my options. Viscount Lacey is not my only living relative, Mary. I shall seek succour from my mother's family."

"But you've told me they wanted nothing to do with her! You know that. What chance then that they might take you into their fold, my dearest?"

"I cannot know. What I do know is that, at the time of my mother's demise, I had a cousin living in Bath. It is my hope that she will acknowledge me. If she will not, well, it doesn't bear thinking about at the moment. Meanwhile, I shall say nothing of this to the viscount. He must believe we are complying with his wishes for the time being, for it's evident he's a man who is accustomed to getting his own way. But you may be very sure I will not be ridden roughshod over. If he thinks he can tell me what to do, he may think again."

The plan that Patience had put forward did not inspire Mary with confidence, but at least she had lost the desperate look that last night had so worried her, and that in itself must be a good thing.

The viscount was ready and waiting for them at the allotted time. He was mounted on a fine-looking bay and invited them to enter the carriage, escorting them for the half-mile ride to the cottage that was to be their temporary home. Upon arrival, he dismounted and saw to the distribution of their belongings before joining them on a tour of the house. It was a fine building in the Tudor style, the rooms being sufficiently spacious without depicting any display of undue grandeur, and Patience loved it immediately.

"I hope you will be comfortable here. You have only to send word up to the Place if there is anything you require. The undercook is to remain with you and I shall not disturb you again today, as I am sure you will wish for some time to settle in. I'll return tomorrow, when we might perhaps discuss how to move forward from here."

Once more, and as demurely as before, Patience thanked him for his kindness. "It is good of you to go to so much trouble on our behalf, sir. We are strangers, after all."

Mary could only be grateful that their host was unacquainted with her friend's normally less than meek disposition. He left them to their own devices and Patience's first act was to summon those members of staff who had been allocated to her.

"Allow me to introduce myself and my companion. I am Miss Worthington, your master's cousin, and this is Miss Petersham. It is good of you to leave your usual duties to undertake our care. No doubt you are as unfamiliar with the house as we are, but I'm sure we shall establish a working routine in no time. Meanwhile, do not hesitate to come to me if you have any questions or if you require provision for something that is not yet here."

The cook wiped her hands on her apron, the maid bobbed a curtsey and the footman stood ready to do anything she might ask of him, for her smile was warm and her manner, though in accordance with her position, was not too high. Patience had always the way of endearing herself to those around her.

"Alice, is it?" she asked, turning to the maid. "Perhaps you could bring us some tea in the parlour before unpacking our trunks. That will be all for now," she continued, addressing them all.

"Would you like me to show you the menu, Miss, in case there's anything you want to change?" the cook asked.

"That won't be necessary. I'm certain that whatever you provide will suit us admirably."

Cook, who was a little nervous at her suddenly elevated position, swelled with pride and vowed to herself to do everything she could to please her ladies.

"Well, now we can begin to feel at ease, don't you think, Mary?" Patience said, relaxing into a chair after they had gone.

"I know you don't care a fig for such things, but I must say you handled that very well."

Patience laughed. "Of course I care, but my behaviour only reflects what you have taught me. These poor people have been dragged away from their duties to serve people of whom they have no knowledge. I would be less than sensitive to their situation if I didn't take their feelings into account."

Mary knew it to be true. Patience may act the hoyden on occasion and certainly she didn't always conform, but there was no-one with a kinder heart. She changed the subject. "I don't suppose you could change your mind about staying here, my dear? It is a delightful house and has everything we could desire."

Patience laughed. "It's true. This is just such a place as I would have chosen myself, but I will not be beholden to that man! He sweeps all before him as if he owns the place."

"He does own it."

Patience put her hand up, as if acknowledging a hit. "But he does not own me. If he were doing what he is out of kindness, I should like it better. But to suffer us out of a sense of duty, for that is what I feel sure is the case, no, insupportable."

Mary knew well there was no doing anything with Patience when she was in such a mood and looked up gratefully as Walter, the footman, came in with the tea.

It was a fine day and Patience stepped outside, curious to see what was attached to her temporary accommodation. She was delighted to find a well-maintained kitchen garden, small but assuredly large enough for their needs. Beyond that a large, enclosed area offered the promise of an abundance of blooms, particularly from the several climbing roses that were attached to the trellis fixed to the walls. *What a pity I won't be here to see them in flower*, she thought, with no little regret. Honesty forced her to admit that here was a place in which she could have been content. Set in the bricks at the far end was an opening which upon inspection she could see led to a wooded area. She wondered if she might at some time have the opportunity to explore, for walking was one of her favourite pastimes.

"Patience, the viscount has just stopped by on his way home," Mary called to her, appearing through the gap in the wall. "You will remember when he left us he was riding. It was just to ask if there was anything we required. I told him you were out here and he declined to remain, but so thoughtful of him, don't you think?"

"Yes, but no great hardship if he was passing the door," she said, unwilling to give anything to this man who she was convinced resented their presence and, honest as ever, whom she could not blame for so doing.

Mary looked disappointed. "You are unjust and that is not like you."

Patience accepted the reprimand, for it was warranted. She linked her arm in that of her mentor and they headed back to the house. "The truth is, Mary, I am conflicted. This place reminds me of the vicarage in so many ways. Except, of course, that it was always filled with people, either those coming to ask advice of my father or friends who would drop in at any time, knowing they could be sure of a welcome. I think that's what I miss most of all, our friends. Nothing this man could do for us can bring any of that back." She halted a moment, her contrition writ clearly on her features. "And I am using him as a recipient for my bad humour, am I not? You are right to scold me, but it does not weaken my resolve. Delightful as it is, a house is not a home without people, and we are not in a position to enlarge our acquaintance here. At Oakenchurch, we were known by all and we had a position in the community. That is not the case here, nor can it ever be in my opinion. Perhaps if his lordship had been a warmer man…"

They'd reached the house and she didn't finish her sentence, but her innate truthfulness caused her to acknowledge the smile in his eyes and those fleeting moments when she had suspected they shared an appreciation of the humour in the situation. No, if he had not been warm, it had been of her own making. It would not do. And she must leave, because the longer she remained the harder it would be to do so.

Her first task upon entering the house was to excuse herself and go to her bedchamber, where she stood at the window pondering on how best she could discover the direction of Clara Buxton in Bath, if indeed she was still there. The solution presented itself almost immediately. She sat down at the small bureau which stood against the wall facing the washstand to write to Mr Wicks, the attorney who had aided her with all the paperwork and legalities that had befallen her upon her father's demise. She would have to ask the viscount to frank the letter for her, something she would have preferred not to do, but this seemed to be the best option if she were to acquire the information she needed. It would take some while, of course, and she resolved to make the best she could of her time at Worthington Place, and that would begin with ceasing to antagonise her host. Feeling more hopeful now, she went in search of Mary. She found her seated in the walled garden with her sketchbook.

"I am recording as much as I can, Patience, for I never saw a place I liked more. It will be nice to have evidence of our time here."

"I think you will have sufficient time to indulge yourself, for I know how you love drawing. Though it is not my wish, I believe we must be fixed here for some while yet to come." She then proceeded to tell Mary what she had done and how she hoped it might ultimately resolve the situation.

CHAPTER THREE

When Gideon arrived the next morning, Patience put on her brightest smile and was surprised to find how easily it came to her.

"Good day, my lord. We must thank you for our accommodation. Mary and I are delighted with the cottage. It reminds us both of home in many ways, for the vicarage was not a large building but spacious and with sufficient rooms for our needs."

He responded in kind, his features transformed when not looking harsh. "I'm so glad to hear you say so. I hope it will continue to please you while we search for a permanent solution to your problem, though you must know you are at liberty to remain here for as long as you wish."

Patience glanced fleetingly at Mary before saying he was very kind and she hoped not to impose on him for too long.

"We are close to Bath here, as I am sure you are aware. When the days grow longer, I shall be happy to escort you to such places as might interest you both. The Abbey is particularly beautiful."

"Yes, I was lucky enough to visit with my father some years ago. I understand the city has many pleasures to offer."

"I know that my mother delights in the shops in Milsom Street, if that's what you mean."

There was an infinitesimal pause when he mentioned the viscountess, but both chose to ignore what might have been a difficult subject and Patience said, "I certainly need to replenish my wardrobe, though it may surprise you to learn I

27

am an adept needlewoman and frequently fashion my own clothes."

"Nothing about you would surprise me, Miss Worthington," he said, laughing out loud. "But we are cousins, and I would suggest we forego all this formality. My given name is Gideon, and with your permission I will use yours."

This was all going rather well and Patience suffered a pang of conscience, but the independent streak in her would not be laid to rest. How easy it would be to remain in this near perfect setting, and how out of the question.

Mary judged it time for her to join in the conversation. "I spent a happy hour yesterday afternoon sitting in the garden with my sketchbook, my lord. Drawing is a particular hobby of mine. I hope you will permit me to indulge myself while we are here."

"By all means. I would have you look upon this as your home."

Patience decided to be open, but without the aggression she had assumed the day before. "Allow me to be frank. My understanding was that you would come here today, my lord … Gideon, to discuss our future. My father left me with a competence which, though not large, I am hoping will be sufficient for my needs. Mary too has some moderate means of her own. We would wish, if at all possible, to attain a small property in Bath from where we might fashion a comfortable life. As you have already pointed out, the city has much to offer."

"I am happy to sponsor you, you must know that."

Patience regarded him in a slightly mocking but inoffensive way. "I'm not sure you would have said as much yesterday, or even if it is the case. It seems your motives are born of duty."

"Is that so bad?"

"No, it does you credit. But I would like you, if you are able, to see it from my point of view. You will already know I have something of an independent nature," she said with something approaching a grin, "and I would prefer if at all possible to stand on my own two feet."

"And yet you were ready to accept support from my father."

"The cases are different. You must see that."

"In all honesty, I do not. I have the means, and it would involve little sacrifice on my part."

"But it would on mine." Her eyes were pleading, hoping so much to make him understand. It seemed he did not.

"It is not my wish to distress you, though it strikes me you are being more than a little stubborn. Let me just say that if you will not accept financial assistance from me, I will do everything in my power to aid you in any other way that I am able."

"You are more than kind, and I fear we must prey on your hospitality for some time to come until Miss Petersham and I can see our way forward."

"Then we shall leave it at that for the time being. Perhaps you will advise me of anything you require." He paused and for a moment looked troubled. "While we are being honest with each other, I must say how regretful it is that I am as yet unable to bring about a reconciliation between you and my mother. It would have given me great pleasure to invite you to the Place when I am entertaining guests, or even for a quiet supper, but all that is out of the question at the moment. We must, I believe, take each day as it comes. Do you ride?" he asked, abruptly changing the subject. "And you, Miss Petersham?"

Patience was taken aback. "Well, yes, I do, though I have had little opportunity. Mary has never acquired the skill and prefers to go out in a carriage, do you not, my dear?" she said, turning to her.

"It is a thing I have always regretted, but I am ashamed to own that I am a little nervous around horses. Such large creatures, they are."

"You are not alone, Miss Petersham. There are many who feel the same way. May I be permitted to take you both driving? I could show you something of the surrounding countryside. And I'm certain there is a mount in the stables that will suit you, Patience, if you care to ride with me."

The prospect filled Patience with excited anticipation, but she was apprehensive too. It would be so easy to become too comfortable here, and that would make it so much more difficult when the time came to leave.

They settled in so well that Mary attempted on more than one occasion to persuade Patience to reconsider their future, to no avail. Perhaps she had inherited that streak of independence that had set her parents on their path all those years ago. Whatever it was, she was determined to carve out a life for herself on her own terms.

While she was waiting, she took advantage of the spring-like weather and the lengthening days to ride out with her cousin. Her old riding habit had to suffice as she could not justify the expenditure of a new one, even if she were to purchase the material and make it herself. It was not this season's fashion, or even last season's, but the blue woollen cloth clung flatteringly to her trim form, and she didn't in any case care for such subtleties. Well, only a little anyway. Gideon took her to the far reaches of his estate and not once did they cover the same ground, save for the initial few minutes. Sometimes they rode in companionable silence and sometimes, at a walking pace, they would each talk of their past. Never did they discuss the future — Patience because she knew it sounded ungracious to be wanting to leave, and Gideon because he was finding increasingly that he didn't want her to go. She learned that he had come into his inheritance at the age of nineteen, when his father had suffered a fatal heart attack.

"I made one or two mistakes, I can tell you, but I was fortunate that my father's steward had been with him from his youth and knows the place inside out."

"There is some good farming land hereabouts, is there not? I used to go walking when my father was busy with his parishioners and learned a little about what conditions will produce the best crop or support the most livestock."

"What an interesting young woman you are, Patience."

She looked at him sideways. "Why should you say so? It was enjoyment to me and a way of keeping in touch with the local folk who were so tied to their work."

Gideon made no reply and, conversation for the time being at an end, they broke into a trot.

At other times, Gideon would drive Patience and Mary along the country lanes, and they had ample opportunity to observe his skill with the reins, some of the roads being in such a state as to challenge even the most competent of drivers. Never had Patience been more content and never had she been more resolved to move forward with her plans, for she had to acknowledge to herself that she was drawn to her cousin far more than was sensible or desirable. Into this almost idyllic existence came a reply from Mr Wicks. He had traced Mrs Buxton's whereabouts. Clara resided in Upper Camden Place with her husband and two children. Patience sat once more at the bureau and, a little reluctantly, wrote to her mother's niece.

My dear Mrs Buxton,

I hope you do not think it an imposition for me to write to you when there is every reason to believe you may not even know of my existence. My name is Patience Worthington and I am your cousin. But allow me to explain. I am sorry to say that many years ago my mother, Elizabeth Longfield, brought scandal to her family. I am not aware of the finer details but it was thought at the time to be sufficient for her to be cut by them entirely, hence my opening to this letter. In all probability her name was never mentioned. It is some years since my mother passed away, my father only recently. She left me a letter to be opened upon his death, and that is how I came to discover both her misdemeanour (though not the details) and the existence of relatives of whom I had been entirely ignorant.

Now comes the hard part, and I must burden you with information which you may not wish to hear. My father, of noble birth but a second son required to earn his living, turned to the church. He was the vicar of a small parish some little distance south of Bath. While he has left me with a small competence, the home which had been mine from birth has passed now to the new incumbent. I am at present residing under the care of Lord Lacey, my father's nephew, but this is a temporary arrangement which I would like to terminate as soon as possible. It is my ambition, along with my friend and companion, Mary Petersham, to establish myself in Bath. However, I am unfamiliar with the city, nor do I have the acquaintanceship of any of its inhabitants, and it is under those circumstances that I would beg you to allow us to come and stay with you for a while to facilitate my plans. I would hope this would not be of long duration, as I am reluctant to inconvenience you. I shall understand, of course, if you wish to have nothing to do with me. Just writing this feels particularly presumptuous, but how will I know if I don't ask?

Yours hopefully
Patience Worthington

She had nothing then to do but wait for a reply.

CHAPTER FOUR

One day while out riding with Gideon, Patience could contain her curiosity no longer. They had dismounted to allow their horses to slake their thirst in a shallow stream and he was leaning against an oak tree, arms folded, while she was seated on the fallen trunk of another. The sun filtered through the surrounding branches, throwing a mottled light down upon the scene.

Patience spoke carefully. "You will forgive me for asking —" would he? — "but you never mention your mother. I hope she is well."

"Quite well, thank you."

She shifted so that she half-faced him and continued. "She must be aware of my presence here, surely. Does she raise no objection?"

"You know, Patience, one of the things I most like about you is your habit of coming straight to the point. No shilly-shallying for you. You want to know if she has demanded that I turn you from my door."

"Something like that, yes."

"I am extremely fond of the viscountess, but it is I and not she who dictates who may stay here."

"But it was because of her that you removed me from Worthington Place to reside at the gatehouse." The words were out before she could stop them, and he laughed.

"Yes, definitely straight to the point. I made that decision on the grounds of expediency. It would have served no purpose to have you remain. With the best will in the world and no matter how hard each of you may have tried to avoid the other, the time would have come when your paths would cross. I don't suppose any of us desires a confrontation or the ignominy should she turn on her heel without a word to you."

"I see your point."

"And naturally I am aware of your distress at the implication regarding your mother's behaviour."

"I was wrong. I know what Lady Lacey said to be the truth of the matter. My mother left me a letter informing me that before her marriage to my father she had behaved badly, though she did not give me any details. It was because of my shock that I behaved in such a way the first day I came here. I regret I did not recant, but that is no excuse for my hot temper."

Gideon was astonished to hear her confession. Regretful too, because things might have been so different. "Do I have your permission to tell my mother what you have said?"

"No, if you don't object. The damage is done. I shall be leaving soon, so there seems little point in raking over the coals."

"What do you mean, you'll be leaving soon?" he said, rather more sharply than he had intended.

"The communication you were so kind as to bring to me yesterday was from my cousin in Bath. My female cousin. On my mother's side. Mary and I are to go to her while we seek a way to settle ourselves. We are invited to stay as long as we please."

Patience had known this would be hard, but she was startled at the violent way he leaped forward and began pacing, going so far as to kick the tree and scuff his boot, something she was certain his valet wouldn't be too pleased about.

"It didn't occur to you to inform me of your actions?" He sounded so cold and she felt her own blood turn to ice.

"You knew what my intention was, for I told you so at the very beginning," she said in a low and slightly unsteady voice.

"And yet you have made no mention of it for some time. I think I can be forgiven for believing you had come to feel you could make your home here. It seems I was mistaken."

How could she explain? That there was no opportunity as matters stood for her to meet and socialise with other people. That the situation between her and the viscount's mother was impossible, and that the fault was her own. That she wanted nothing more than to remain. No. A wall had descended between them. Maybe it was for the best.

They returned to the cottage in silence, and he waited only to see her safely inside before leaving without another word. Thankful that Mary was nowhere to be seen, she raced to her bedchamber and flung herself on the bed, her pent-up emotions giving way to a flood of tears.

Gideon would have preferred to have galloped back to the Place, but the distance was short, his horse was tired and he had to lead Patience's mount back to the stables. In the few minutes it took to reach his destination, his mind was flooded with thoughts he would have preferred to keep at bay. She was leaving. Why had he not foreseen this? What a wilful woman she was! Had she not been a thorn in his side since the day she'd arrived, a responsibility he had not sought? He would be better off without her.

An hour later, newly changed into more suitable raiment, he entered the drawing room to greet his mother. "Good day, Mama. I trust your arthritis is bothering you less now that the weather has improved."

It was a good effort, but she had known him from birth, had soothed his hurt when a child and wiped away his tears. The only time she had seen such a look on his face was when he was severely troubled. "What is it, my son? Something has occurred to put you out of countenance."

"Heavens, no. You are imagining things. I am well enough."

Whatever it was that bothered him, it was evident he wasn't readily going to confide in her. She would have to find out by other means, so she allowed him to talk, trusting all would become clear in due course.

"I think perhaps I will take a bolt to town before the hot weather sets in. Adam writes that he is still there, and I haven't seen him in an age. Would you care to come with me?"

"Is this not sudden? I had no notion you were thinking along those lines."

"I have been considering for a while that I should go. If for nothing else, I am sorely in need of a visit to my tailor," he said, smiling.

She wasn't fooled. "I think perhaps I will remain at the Place. There is always Bath closer by, should I become bored, but I am quite content at present. And what of your visitor?"

He made the mistake of feigning indifference. "My visitor?"

"The young woman who is staying at the gatehouse. Lizzie Longfield's daughter. You have said nothing, but I know she has been there for some time."

"You are right, of course, but I felt it my duty to accommodate her as I am certain my father would have done. But she will be leaving shortly. She has other relations to whom she has applied, so you will not run the risk of encountering her while I am gone."

So that was what accounted for the desolate look in her son's eyes. She sighed inwardly, thinking perhaps it was time she made the acquaintance of Miss Patience Worthington. Not a decision she would confide to Gideon. Instead, she asked him when he planned to go and suggested there were one or two errands he might run for her while he was away. He said that naturally he would be delighted and went off to collect his gun to see if he could grab a brace of rabbits while there was still sufficient daylight. Well, at least that would give him something upon which to vent his obvious frustration.

Patience had wiped her tears and once more taken up the letter she had received from Clara Buxton.

My dearest Patience,

You cannot know what a delight it was for me to receive your letter. Buxton has gone into the country to deal with some matters on the estate. He has taken the boys with him — I have two. Seven and five years of age and much better off in a place where they can climb trees or swim in the river, though I miss them greatly. I spend the better part of my time here rather than at the manor, but between you and me I am grown a trifle bored. Of course you must come and stay. And Mary too.

You are right, of course. I had no knowledge of your existence, or indeed that of my aunt. Presumably her name has been expunged entirely from the family records. Well, I'm sure most families have a scandal of some sort or another that they wish to hide from prying eyes. Do not feel you need to make your visit fleeting. You have confided to me something of your circumstances and only think how much more convenient, if we are to go about together, that we are residing under the same roof. You must not feel it necessary to set up your own establishment with any haste.

You do not mention your age, but I am surmising that you are younger than I. I am six and twenty. If you are not averse to the suggestion, we must make it our business to find a husband for you. Life is that much easier for a married lady, don't you think, and I am so happy with Buxton. Oh dear, I have just thought. You are not a blue-stocking, are you? I am not bookish myself, though I do occasionally make use of the lending library. My goodness, how I am rambling on. Let me end then by saying I will have rooms in readiness for you and Mary, and you may come at any time that is convenient to you. My home is in Upper Camden Place. The full direction is at the top of this page. Come soon, if you will. I cannot wait to meet you and to show you all the delights that Bath has to offer.

With affection
Clara Buxton

Patience could not help picking up some of the excitement from the page before her. Clara's enthusiasm was infectious, even in the written word. It was what she needed, for there was no doubt it would be a wrench to tear herself away from Worthington Place. In the few weeks she had been there, her resentment of her host had given way to deep contentment with her current lot. Well, she had always known it was but a temporary interlude. It was time to move on. She went to find Mary, who had not yet seen the letter, to discuss when and how they should make the move.

Patience didn't look for Gideon the next morning at the time of their habitual ride. She was as certain as she could be that he wouldn't come, so angry had he been the previous day, but nothing could have astonished her more than a note, delivered by the footman, summoning her to the Place. The note was not from the viscount but from his mother.

Patience walked the half mile with her heart thumping in her breast. What could this woman, who had thus far refused even to meet her, possibly want with her now? She was shown into a comfortable drawing room, not overly large, decorated and upholstered in a light blue which was both pleasing to the eye and relaxing to the nerves. This was, she felt sure, Lady Lacey's private domain. The woman herself was seated in an armchair that seemed almost to swallow her whole, so diminutive was she. Patience had prepared herself for a woman of considerable stature, for her son was large-framed though elegant withal.

"Forgive me if I do not rise. Sadly, my limbs no longer do what I would wish of them. Do please be seated. Patience, isn't it?"

"It is, Lady Lacey. Before I sit, I must tell you that I will shortly be leaving Worthington Place, so if it is your intention to dismiss me it will not be necessary."

"Come down from that high place and do as you are bid. I have not asked you to come only to send you away, but to apologise."

Patience almost fell into the chair and sat facing her aunt in astonishment and with no little curiosity. Could this pleasantly spoken woman be the one she had raised in her mind to the status of ogress?

"You are surprised. Small wonder, after the way I treated you before. Allow me to tell you, incidentally, that you are the image of your mother. You have Lizzie's outspoken manner too. No, don't look like that. It was one of the things I most liked about her."

It seemed only fair that she should make her own admission. "I too must apologise, for I was less than honest with your son. Though I didn't know the circumstances, I was aware that my mother had in some way behaved unacceptably, for she advised me of it herself in a letter I received long after her death. I found it so hard to accept, for I grew up in the presence of a couple who could not have been more in love. Denial seemed the only way forward for me, if all my memories were not to be tarnished. But it doesn't pay to run from the truth, does it?"

Hester Worthington rather thought that running from the truth might be exactly what she was doing now. She forbore saying so, however, merely telling her visitor she was hopeful of making good the time they had lost. "You are not leaving immediately, I trust?"

"Within a few days, I think."

"Then perhaps you would dine with me before you go. And the lady who came with you, I'm afraid I don't know her name."

"Mary Petersham. She was my governess but has for some years been my companion and friend. I fear your son will not wish me to join you. We have fallen out, I'm afraid. It is kind of you to ask me, though, and I appreciate it more than I can say."

"You need not worry about Gideon. He has this morning left for London, and I don't know when he will return. Come, what harm can it do? I will, if I can, tell you something of your mother. We were the best of friends until, well, until the scandal. And you can tell me of your plans, if you don't think I am being unacceptably inquisitive."

So Gideon had gone. And without even saying goodbye. How fortunate she'd had the wit to take her future into her own hands.

"In that case I should be delighted, as I know Mary will be too."

"Tomorrow then, if it suits you."

"I shall look forward to it, Lady Lacey."

"I prefer that you call me Aunt Hester. We are related, are we not?"

Patience walked very slowly back to the gatehouse. She had much to think about. She had warmed to her aunt almost immediately, the old vision fast disappearing, and she admitted to herself that she would like to learn more of her mother's girlhood. Uppermost in her mind, though, was that Gideon had left without a word. She could not deny the hurt she felt, but nor could she blame him. Would it have been such a bad thing to have taken him into her confidence? Well, it was all too late to be thinking of that now. In a few days she would be gone and never have to see him again. It was with a heavy heart that she arrived back at the cottage.

CHAPTER FIVE

Gideon had chosen to drive himself in his curricle, his luggage following in another carriage accompanied by his valet. He preferred to use his own horses and, consequent upon the need to rest them up, he engaged lodgings on the way. It was thus a few days before he reached London. Having sent word ahead, he arrived to find his town house in readiness, the Holland covers having been removed and his servants ready to gratify his every whim.

His protracted journey had given him plenty of time to think, and to regret his hasty departure from Worthington Place. Gideon's disappointment at his cousin's revelation had turned swiftly to an anger, which at first he didn't question. Over time, though, he realised his reaction had been disproportionate, and he sought to find a reason for it. By the time he arrived in Grosvenor Square, he had his answer. In just a few weeks of knowing her, he had fallen hopelessly in love with Patience. It was an emotion so novel to him that it had gone unrecognised and therefore unacknowledged. *Just as well I didn't stay to take my leave of her*, he thought. *I might then have made a complete cake of myself.*

He looked back upon all those times they had been riding together. There was no doubt she had enjoyed these outings as much as he had. No-one could feign that degree of pleasure for such a prolonged period and in any case, had it not been so, she could easily have rejected his invitations. They had fallen into an easy habit of conversation, and so much had he delighted in their time together he had taken its continuance for granted, not questioning the future. The shock then, when it came, had been all the greater.

"Good afternoon, my lord, and welcome home," the butler had said upon his arrival.

"Thank you, Sarratt, it's good to be here," Gideon said, laying his whip and gloves on a small table in the entrance hall and placing his hat and cape in the man's waiting hands.

"We weren't sure when you would arrive, but I know Auguste is keen to serve up some of your favourite delights," Sarratt remarked, smiling with the familiarity of one who had known his master from a child.

"Then inform him, please, that I shall dine at home this evening and will come to the table with an appetite that only a day on the road can bring about. Has Chadlington arrived yet?"

"He has, my lord, and my understanding is that your luggage is already unpacked."

"In that case, I shall see if I can't shake off some of this dust and with his help appear attired to do justice to the many treats my chef no doubt has in store for me." He took the stairs two at a time and speedily reached the sanctuary of his dressing room. Chadlington was waiting for him, and he allowed the man to help him off with his boots and coat before dismissing him to lie for a while on the bed in the adjacent chamber, hands clasped behind his head and staring up at the ceiling.

A few hours later he dined in splendid isolation and retired early, too tired to seek out friends at his club, which had been his original intention. His contemplation of the ceiling resumed but brought him no more comfort that it had earlier. Giving it up, he turned on his side, crooked his elbow and shoved his arm beneath his cheek. Sleep was a long time in coming. He couldn't help wondering if Patience had yet left for Bath and what delights she might be enjoying — without him

"Invited us to dine with her!" Mary had exclaimed when Patience had told her of Lady Lacey's solicitation. "After all these weeks! You said no, of course."

"No, I accepted very graciously, just as you have taught me." Patience's grin was impossible to hide before she continued, more seriously, "I think it is to her credit that she has made the first move, something I could never have done under the circumstances. Perhaps it was just the shock of us arriving uninvited and the memories it must have induced. And I was touched when she said how much I look like Mama."

"We knew that already."

"Not in the same way. You didn't meet her until she was some years older, and my memories of when I was a child have blurred with how I saw her later. The viscountess obviously perceived something that reminded her of my mother as a much younger woman. She was, after all, only eighteen years of age when last they met."

"When you put it that way, it must have come as something of a shock to her."

"I believe it did."

"So we are to dine with her tomorrow? She invites me too?"

"I wish you will get over this habit you have of regarding yourself as being still in employment, Mary. You are my dear friend, and I could not have come through the loss of either of my parents with fortitude had you not been at my side."

"Old habits die hard, Patience."

"Well, it's time this one was buried."

Both young women dressed carefully the following day and presented themselves at the allotted time. They were escorted directly to the dining room, where Lady Lacey joined them a few minutes later. She walked with a stick and it was evident that she was in considerable discomfort.

"Forgive an old lady. I do not get around as well as I used to. Good evening, Patience. And Mary, may I call you Mary? Sit down, girls, for I most certainly must do so." She was disarming, that was for sure. She could not yet have attained her fiftieth birthday, but her disability had put years on her, as she explained to them. "Sadly I was thrown from my horse, and I can tell you that more than my pride was hurt that day. I never fully recovered and it is of all things what I miss most, riding." She seemed to drag herself back to the present day from a long ago memory. "However, I didn't ask you here to talk about me but to explain, if I can, how Lizzie and I came to fall out. But first we will eat," she said as the servants came into the room.

They spoke only of innocuous things until the meal was over and they could be private again.

"Oblige me, Patience, by taking my arm and we shall retire to my drawing room where I saw you yesterday. It is the place I am most comfortable."

As they sat, the two younger women faced her with such an intense look of enquiry on both their faces that she laughed, and that did much to relieve the tension.

"You should see yourselves," she said, "both sitting bolt upright, as if in the schoolroom and expecting to be reprimanded. Relax and I shall tell you what I can." She took a deep breath and began. "Lizzie and I had been friends almost since birth. Our homes were adjacent. We were of an age. It would have been strange had we not struck up a close friendship under those circumstances. She was always more vivacious than I, always wanting to be doing. Where I was content to sew my sampler, she would be gazing out of the window, looking longingly at the trees she so obviously wanted to climb. I told her often that she should have been born a boy."

Patience leaned forward, fascinated by this side of her mother she'd never known.

"We shared a governess. I think our parents thought we might be encouraged to learn if there were two of us together. I'm not sure that worked, but it was assuredly more pleasant for us to have a companion. We were so different, but it seemed not to matter. And so we grew to adulthood." She paused for a moment, as though gathering her thoughts. "There was a bond between us that I would have sworn none could break, but then came Lord Lacey upon the scene. He was some years older than me, but with so much charm. My son has inherited it, as I'm sure you will have noticed."

Patience remained silent.

"Lizzie was confined to the house with something contagious when first I met him. By the time she was back in circulation my fate was sealed, but I had not seen her for weeks and had been unable to confide in her. Forgive me, child, but what I have to say next must of necessity distress you. My husband was a handsome man, and she set her cap at him. It wasn't surprising that she too fell for his charm, but it seemed she lost all sense of propriety in striving to win him. Our betrothal had not yet been announced but everyone close to us, excepting your mother of course, knew how things stood between us. We were at a large social gathering when she finally came to understand the situation. I watched as her eyes opened wide. Then she did something very ill-advised and said loudly and in a voice that cut through other conversations that she hoped we would be very happy together — and then she stormed out of the room."

"Oh no!"

"I'm afraid so, my dear. There was no hiding what had happened. Her own family were so ashamed of her that they kept her from the public eye. Only your father, who it seems was as enraptured by her as she had been by Charles, saved her from herself. My understanding is that he called every day and finally persuaded her to marry him. The brothers fell out, each so protective of the woman they loved. Lizzie and Nicholas were married quietly and moved away. That is the story in a nutshell."

The silence that followed her tale stretched into the distance before Patience rose and walked to the window. She came back and knelt beside Hester.

"My poor aunt. And my poor mother. How sad that you should have been estranged all those years, and how stupid of her to have allowed her emotions to so colour her future. I cannot be entirely sorry, though, for I must tell you that my parents were idyllically happy, as it is obvious you and my uncle were. Perhaps, once the passion of youth had worn off, she came to appreciate what she had. I know for certain that she never regretted her marriage to my father."

"Then perhaps we can all be at peace."

"I am grateful to you, Aunt Hester, for I would never otherwise have known the full story and must always have wondered. It seems my mother was a headstrong and foolish young girl, but her parents have a lot to answer for, cutting her off from Society as they did. They would have done better to brazen it out. People would have forgotten soon enough after your marriage, I am sure. As it was, it would seem they acknowledged her guilt and therefore others would too. Was there no compassion?"

"Too often in this life people are more concerned about the opinions of others than the sentiments of those closest to them. When they cut off their daughter they cut me too, as though I also had been at fault. Remember, if you will, that I had been in and out of their home as a child almost as if it were my own. I married and came here and never saw them again. I carried my anger against Lizzie down through the years and it wasn't until after you came here, after I excluded you, that I realised how futile such actions are. And that is why I asked you to come and see me. I hope it is not too late for us to have some kind of familial relationship."

"I should like that of all things, but you must know that I am leaving very soon."

"I do know, of course, but Bath is no great distance from here. While I cannot journey to visit you there, I hope you will find the time to come and see me now and then. It would make me very happy."

Patience embraced her aunt. Mary, who had remained silent throughout, drew out her handkerchief and dried her tears.

"Well, I'll be dashed! What the devil brings you to town?" Adam Conway said, wringing Gideon's hand when he came upon him in the street.

"My tailor, old boy. What else?"

Both laughed and, linking arms, continued by mutual consent to their club only a short distance away.

"You couldn't have timed your visit better. There's a horse I'm thinking of buying. Wouldn't mind your opinion. He's up to my weight all right, but there's something I'm not quite sure about."

"If he's up to your weight, he must stand well over sixteen hands."

"I always was on the large side," Adam said, running his free hand over his ample stomach. "Never could resist a decent plate of food."

"Or two."

"Don't hold back, will you?"

Gideon began to feel better about his decision to come to London, even if it had been a hasty one. A disturbed night had brought him to the conclusion that there was little option but to put all thoughts of Patience aside and move on. Easier said than done, but what other choice did he have? There was much entertainment to be had at this time of year, and he was resolved to enter into everything that was on offer. Adam wasn't his only close friend in the town, and he did need to visit his tailor. Hoby's too, for the acquisition of new boots had also become a priority.

Before too long, news of Lord Lacey's arrival had reached the ears of those ladies with daughters of a marriageable age who were looking for a good catch, and they didn't come much better than Gideon Worthington. He received all manner of invitations, ranging from informal suppers and soirées through to formal balls. He wasn't a vain man and was flattered to be included, sometimes at very short notice when hostesses learned he was in town. He was happy to do the pretty with the young ladies to whom he was introduced, but he was careful to raise no false hopes in any maiden's breast. He was, he decided, destined to remain a bachelor for, try though he might, he could not get Patience out of his mind.

A few weeks later, he was to receive news of her at a supper given by Adam. "Just a small affair," he had told his visitors, "but my chef is second to none, and it feels wrong to keep him all to myself."

All four men present were known to one and other, so a convivial evening was a foregone conclusion. One was Adam's brother, Oliver, and the other Freddie Hildebrand, Gideon's oldest friend, whom he hadn't seen since his arrival in London, something he commented upon.

"Only got here yesterday, old boy. Been to see my uncle. You know, the one who's as rich as Croesus."

"Turning him up sweet were you, Freddie?"

"No such thing, Adam. Besides, I'm his closest relation. Bound to leave it all to me when he kicks the bucket."

"In that case, I shall know where to come if I find myself in difficulties."

This caused some mirth, as their host was very well-heeled and unlikely to need rescuing from penury, any more than Freddie himself, and all were aware that he was excessively fond of the old man.

"Thought the place would be filled with people in their dotage, but it was quite lively. Plenty to do, and I stayed longer than I'd intended. Even took the waters. Evil stuff. In fact, Adam, I need some more of that fine Burgundy, because just the thought of it brings back the taste."

Gideon looked up quickly, the mention of the waters rousing his interest. "You've come from Bath?"

"Isn't that what I said, Lacey? In fact, I met some sort of connection of yours. Well, I presume she was. A Miss Worthington. Staying with the Buxtons. A fine-looking young woman, I must say, though I didn't get close to her. Surrounded, she was, and from the glimpses I caught I could see why."

"Yes, a cousin of mine." He hesitated before asking, nonchalantly he hoped, "And did she seem to be enjoying herself?"

"Couldn't tell you. Like I said, I didn't get anywhere near her. I only know her name because my companion told me. He said she was the latest craze."

Gideon was reduced to silence, and the fine dishes presented by his host's chef turned to ashes in his mouth. While managing to maintain his part in the conversation, he mind was running along very different lines from those being discussed. Only when they sat down later to play cards could he relax a little, the need for talk subsiding as they all concentrated on their hands. A rush of envy came over him at the idea of others paying court to Patience, but his kinder nature took over. After all, if she wasn't interested in him, at least it was to be hoped that among her suitors she would find one to assure her future. Somehow, though, the thought didn't comfort him.

CHAPTER SIX

It was with a heavy heart that Patience had left Worthington Place, something she would not admit even to herself. It wasn't in her nature to dwell on misfortune, and she chose rather to focus on what lay before her. There could be no doubt, however, that the promise she had made to her aunt — assuring her that she would visit soon — brought as much comfort to her as it did to its recipient.

"I cannot wait to meet my cousin," she said to Mary as she sank back against the cushions in Hester Worthington's private carriage, taken at her aunt's insistence. "Was it not kind of Lady Lacey to lend us such luxurious transport?"

Mary, leaving with her own feelings of regret, for she had been so very happy living in the gatehouse, realised immediately that Patience was putting on a brave front and responded accordingly. And so it was that they chatted excitedly all the way to Upper Camden Place and arrived to such an unreserved welcome that the anxiety both had been experiencing fell away immediately.

"My dearest Patience," exclaimed Clara, running down the steps and crushing her in an embrace even as she stepped from the carriage. "I have been longing for this moment since first it was confirmed that you were coming. And Mary," she said expansively. "Come in, come in." With which she led them into the house, talking all the way and pausing only when they entered a beautifully appointed morning room where no expense had been spared to make its occupants comfortable. "Right, let me look at you," she said as she turned to face the two other women. She grasped her cousin's hands and drew in a deep breath. "Well! I should have known you anywhere. You have exactly the look of my poor departed mother. I favour my father, you know." Patience was astonished to see her brush away a tear, surprised to see such emotion in one so ebullient, but Clara was herself again almost immediately. "You must forgive me. It was the shock. Well, let us sit down. I shall order some tea and we shall spend just a while together, to get to know each other, you understand, before I show you to your bedchambers. I shall take you myself, for I want to make sure you are both pleased with what I have arranged for you. After that, I have decided that we will stay at home this evening, not that I am suggesting you are tired after so short a journey, but because it will be an opportunity for me to tell you of some of the plans I have made for you and for you to advise me of anything you should like to do that I have omitted to mention."

Clara, it seemed, rarely felt the need to pause for breath, but though she talked animatedly and at length, there was no doubt that this was not an empty-headed creature but one of acuity. Patience, who had liked her on sight, saw no reason to change her opinion.

In what seemed no time at all, Patience and Mary were swept into a world they had never before experienced. Though both were eligible by birth to move in such circles, circumstances had thus far precluded either from doing so. It was true that Patience had enjoyed the hospitality of the squire and other families living in the vicinity of the vicarage, and in recent years so had Mary. They had even participated in the occasional local dance, and a natural aptitude dispelled any nerves Patience might otherwise have suffered. But socialising on this scale was both exciting and, in many ways, formidable. Without the support and knowledge of their hostess, the two young women might have fared very differently.

"The first thing we must do tomorrow is examine your wardrobes. It will be fatal to your success should you not be suitably attired," Clara had told them earnestly on that first evening.

Patience recalled her less than fashionable riding habit and knew she would not be wearing it again. Perhaps it was just as well, as it reminded her painfully of her time with Gideon and a life she would not admit she longed for. It was Mary who was bold enough to say, "Neither of us is well-endowed, Clara. I'm afraid we must develop a certain circumspection."

The tinkling laugh rang out. It was a sound they were to hear often, and it never palled.

"You would be amazed at what little tricks we might employ to disguise a once or twice worn gown with some ribbon here or some feathers there. Besides, we are all of a size. Buxton scolds me when I tell him I am not the girl I once was…" She looked away and a smile lifted the corners of her mouth as she dwelt upon some private thought, before bringing herself back to the task in hand. "But the truth is that even after two children, I am still able to wear dresses I had when we were first married. Now, where was I? Ah, yes. I have trunks of gowns that I've never been able to bring myself to throw away. Some are so dated that they will never see the light of day again, but there are others that my dressmaker will not be too proud to refurbish. I'm so glad you have come. I haven't been this diverted for ages, and to tell you the truth I have been missing Buxton dreadfully, but I shall write and tell him he may remain as long as he needs to finish his business without worrying about me dwindling into a decline."

Patience's eyes met Mary's in a smile of pure joy. Neither could imagine Clara ever having time to indulge in low spirits, for it was evident her mind would always be racing on to the next thing. It was, however, a situation entirely unacceptable to her visitors.

"Clara, I am sure I may speak for Mary as well when I say we cannot impose upon you so far. My conscience is already pricking me, but if there is one thing I can do, and do well, it is fashion my own clothes. If you will just escort the two of us to a suitable warehouse, we can avail ourselves of all the materials we need to turn ourselves out in style."

"She's right, you know, and I think you'll discover you cannot move her once she has made up her mind."

They had reckoned without their hostess. The laugh came again. "Then we shall compromise. For a start, nothing would give me more pleasure than to be rummaging around in any number of warehouses, but you must allow me to adhere to my first suggestion in some part. It shall be you, Patience, and not my dressmaker, who makes the alterations, but I truly do have numerous articles that are longing for that special touch, a little imagination. It makes no sense to buy everything new under such circumstances. And, though I intend to show you all of Bath's delights and to introduce you to my friends and acquaintance, we cannot all the while be on the go. We shall spend some time at our needlework. Well, you will, for I have no application at all, but I am very good at suggestions and am able to visualise clearly how something will turn out. Is it agreed, then?"

Both Patience and Mary knew when they were beaten, and the scheme was acceded to. When Clara discovered Mary's aptitude for and love of drawing, she begged her to sketch a portrait of her as a surprise for her husband when he should eventually return to Bath. Thus all three would be companionably occupied at those times when they remained at home and no visitors were present. They dined together before retiring to face a new life the next day. If the evening was anything to judge by, it was evident they would, all three, get along famously.

"I couldn't possibly accept, Clara! It's absolutely beautiful."

It had indeed caused Clara a pang to offer the gown to Patience, but she was nothing if not generous. It was quite a formal dress of green silk and had only been worn on one occasion.

"You must, or you will break my heart. It is quite a favourite of mine, but for some reason it does unacceptable things to the tone of my skin. The only time I wore it, at the Monkton ball it was, all my friends kept asking if I felt quite the thing and perhaps I should take a turn on the terrace if I was too hot. It was no such thing, of course, but I've never been able to bring myself even to try it on again."

"But surely, if we were to attach some cream lace to the neckline and the cuffs, it would resolve the situation. It's only when directly against your throat and arms that the problem occurs, I presume."

"Patience is right, Clara. With a little ingenuity, we could make it perfect for you."

"No, my mind is made up, Mary. See, even as she holds it across her arms it lights up her face."

There was no denying it, and so Patience tried it on and her cousin beamed with joy. No alteration was necessary. It might have been made for her. Emerald green silk on creamy alabaster skin, clear grey eyes and straw-coloured hair, the classic look was perfection.

"You have the air of a Greek goddess, dearest. I am almost glad it does not suit me and even more so that I didn't dispose of it."

"I hardly think I shall have occasion to wear such a dress," Patience said, looking at her reflection in the glass. She was a modest girl in so far as her appearance was concerned, but she could not help being pleased at what she saw.

"Nonsense. There will be many such occasions. Now, Mary, it's your turn," she said, rummaging around in the large trunk that she'd had placed in the centre of her dressing room. "Yes, this one, I think." She turned triumphantly to face the other two and held up against herself a simple gown of pale gold embroidered with thread of the same colour. It was eminently suitable for a woman not in the first blush of youth and Clara had discarded it, thinking it too old for her, though of course she didn't tell Mary that. It would complement her brownish hair and eyes.

One gown after another was cast aside. The trunk was removed to be replaced by one even larger. On the bed lay the dresses that had been chosen, a small pile of those that needed no alteration and a larger pile where ribbons, lace and other enhancements were considered to be desirable. The trunk was taken away, together with those garments Clara had discarded on the carpet. There could be no doubt that of them all their hostess had most enjoyed the afternoon's activity. She made it impossible for either Patience or Mary to refuse her, even had they wanted to.

"Well, I think there is plenty for you to be getting on with, don't you?" she said, smiling at her cousin. "Tomorrow, no, the next day, we shall go into town and indulge in some shopping. I am certain you will be delighted with what there is on offer. Such a wealth of establishments for us to choose from. And I know the very place to purchase some ribbon to match that yellow muslin. But first, a trip to the Pump Room. You cannot be above forty-eight hours in Bath without a visit to the Pump Room!"

Memories came flooding back to Patience as they walked into the Abbey Church Yard and for a moment she was caught off guard, so overwhelmed by thoughts of her father that she had to bite her lip in an attempt to hide her distress from her companions.

"What is it, dearest?" asked Clara, aware immediately of her change of mood. "You look as though you have seen a ghost."

Patience had been unprepared for the rush of emotion and for a moment looked this way and that, as if unsure of herself. "In a way, I have. You may remember I mentioned that I came here once with my father. It wasn't long after my mother passed away and he was only just coming to terms, if indeed he ever did, with his loss. He found some solace in the Abbey, I know. I did myself. There was a peace that pervaded all, and it's my belief it was a compelling moment for him. Forgive me, I didn't expect to have such a strong reaction coming here again. If only I'd thought."

"Would you prefer that we forego our visit to the Pump Room and go there instead?"

Patience marvelled at her cousin's sensitivity. This seemingly frivolous woman hid a heart of gold, and Patience could only be glad she'd had the courage to apply to her, though she was increasingly experiencing feelings of conscience at the obligation which, for the time being at least, she saw no way of diminishing or repaying. "No, not at all, Clara. I would choose to come another day, when I've had more time to prepare myself. In any case, I have long been waiting to see this place that, if hearsay is correct, is the hub of Bath's activities."

"Yes, its reputation has been built to such a degree that I shall be disappointed not to find the whole of Society in this one place," added Mary.

"Maybe not that, Mary, but certainly it is a place to see and, as importantly, to be seen. Ah, there is Mrs Sacombe," Clara said, lowering her voice as they entered. "As meddlesome a woman as you could wish to meet, though endearing, but her approval is essential if you are to be a success."

"I'm not here to be a success," Patience said, her indignation quite evident.

"Then I shall wash my hands of you, for never was there a young woman who was more possessed of those attributes necessary to ensure her future. Except your lack of fortune, of course, but that makes it even more imperative that you do not hinder your chances. Now smile prettily, for I am about to introduce you."

Clara approached the matronly woman without preamble, and the introductions were made. Mrs Sacombe, whose forbidding stature and direct stare had on occasion put more than one person in a flap, chose to be entertained, this being attributable in no small measure to the respectful but assured way in which both Patience and Mary exchanged greetings with her.

"We are always happy to welcome visitors to Bath. Do you stay long?"

"In truth, I know not. Our plans are not entirely formulated. My cousin has been kind enough to extend her invitation until such time as we have a clearer idea as to whether or not we will remain in the area. I am recently left without either parent and must choose my own path in future. I am fortunate I have the advantage of Mrs Buxton's experience and advice."

"You could do worse. I suggest you allow her now to make you known to more of her friends. She has a large acquaintance, and your connection to her will open many doors. Come and visit me when you are more settled. Clara will give you my direction."

It was said more in the spirit of a command than an invitation and with no little condescension, but they thanked her prettily before moving away. Patience and Mary had a few moments in which to survey their surroundings before they were seemingly surrounded. The room was long and elegant, housing a dais at one end above which was a gallery, where sat a band which Clara informed them was in daily attendance. On three sides were set Corinthian columns, and in the centre of the south side a marble vase from which the famous waters issued. It was a handsome place of pleasing proportions, and the two women had no cause to wonder why it was so popular a venue. Even at such an early hour it was already crowded, and the rest of the morning went by in a whirl as one introduction after another was made. Most were residents of Bath, some were visitors.

"It seems Society is represented here in every guise, Clara."

"It is above all what makes it so interesting. Old ladies with their companions, often a poor relation. Oh dear, that's not what I meant at all." But Patience only laughed and her cousin continued. "You will see men courting pretty young girls, others on the lookout for an heiress ingratiating themselves with fond mamas. Military gentlemen. Those who come to take the water in the hope it will cure some ailment or other. There is no better place to observe life than the Pump Room, and I confess it has kept me amused for hours at a time. So you see, do you not, why this was where I wanted to bring you first."

As the minutes went by, Patience acknowledged that Clara knew exactly what she was talking about. If one were at all mischievous, and she was definitely that, one could be hugely entertained watching the antics of people who were unaware of one's attention. All were keen to engage with their fellows, the ruses that were employed sometimes subtle, sometimes blatant. By the time the ladies again attained the relative tranquillity of Upper Camden Place, their knowledge of Bath Society was much increased, and if thoughts of companionable rides with Gideon intruded from time to time, well, that would soon pass, Patience was sure.

CHAPTER SEVEN

"Is that the knocker again?" asked Clara, looking up from where she was studying Mary's drawing. "It seems never to be still these days."

If the words sounded complaining, they belied the sentiment behind them. Mrs Buxton was having a wonderful time. In the few weeks since her visitors had arrived, life had become a whirl such as she hadn't experienced since before her children were born.

Mary laid her sketchbook aside, for it was to her a private thing, but she knew Clara was pleased with the way her portrait was coming along. She wasn't a woman who could falsely affect the delight she so obviously felt and, though she found it difficult to sit still, always wanting to see what progress was being made, Mary took a great deal of pleasure in her enjoyment. She was not, however, comfortable with showing her work to other people, particularly in the early stages. She was in fact a talented artist, and Clara secretly harboured an ambition to put her in the way of some of her friends who might like to have their own image portrayed. A room had already been allocated in the house where an easel had been set up and where Miss Petersham spent many a happy hour with her watercolours. She had even shown her hostess those sketches she had made while residing at the gatehouse at Worthington Place.

Patience also put her work away, saying, "I shall never get the frill sewn at this rate, and I was so hoping to wear this muslin dress tomorrow," but Clara's laugh tinkled as all three rose to greet the visitors who were just then shown into the drawing room.

"Mr Easton, how delightful to see you again," she said, a slight emphasis on the last word giving away, to her companions at least, her amusement at his determined pursuit of her cousin, for he visited on the slightest pretext and often on none at all. "And you have brought Major Saxby with you. Do be seated, and I will ring for some tea. You can stay, can you not?"

"No, no. I met Major Saxby at the door. Th-thank you, tea would be delightful. I was wondering if you would like to join me for a walk in Sydney Gardens in the morning. It seems a pity not to be t-taking advantage of this f-fine weather. Have you had occasion to visit the gardens yet, Miss Worthington?"

Simon Easton was a young man of some two and twenty summers who had no sooner set eyes on Patience than he made her the object of his gallantry. It was obvious that he was badly smitten and she didn't have the heart to depress his pretensions, for he was in the throes of his first love and it would be no difficult thing to destroy every vestige of confidence, not that he had much of that, to be sure. All the more reason to be compassionate. He looked so earnest that Patience was careful not to look at her cousin for fear of giggling inappropriately, but she had a kind heart and said without hesitation, "A lovely idea, sir. I haven't yet, and it is something I have been wanting to do ever since I came to Bath."

Fortunately Major Saxby, that worthy suitor from Oakenchurch and a much more assured gentleman, professed a wish to be included in the excursion, much to the relief of the ladies. Poor Mr Easton had a tendency either to be loquacious in the extreme and tie himself up in knots or to fall into spells of silence when he had seemingly nothing to say. It made for difficult conversation, but the major could be relied upon to ensure the experience would be enjoyable, and all three ladies looked forward with pleasure to the following day.

"It is good to see you living up to your name. You have such patience with Mr Easton. There are others who would not tolerate his adoration with as much sympathy. It does you credit."

"Not at all, Clara. I have no brothers myself, but there were two or three youths at home whom I had occasion to meet and I was able to observe what a painful age it is for a young man."

"You seem to have an understanding with Major Saxby, my dear?"

There was no doubting the question in her voice and Patience satisfied her curiosity. "He has always been very attentive and I know my father hoped we would make a match of it, but I'm afraid the understanding is all on his side. He is solid and reliable, and I am delighted to find him in Bath where as yet I have so few friends, but marriage? No. He is aware of my sentiments, for he has on more than one occasion solicited my hand. Poor man, I believe he thinks he will wear me down in time. Mary describes him as being worthy, do you not?" she said, turning to her. Mary was so engrossed in her drawing that she didn't even know she was being addressed, and Patience let it pass. "I cannot fault him if I list his attributes. We were raised in the same village. He has had an exemplary career in the army, from which he is now retired. He owns a tidy property quite close to the vicarage so, were I to marry him, I would always be among friends. He is kind. He is generous. And yes, Clara, he is worthy." She smiled, but her face expressed an appeal that her cousin might understand. "I am only two and twenty years old. Naturally I hope one day to find a man I can be happy with, but until then I crave a little excitement. You may imagine that the life of a vicar's daughter was of necessity restrained. Will you just listen to me?" she said, aghast at herself. "Here I am, having a wonderful time, my days and evenings filled with new experiences, and I am complaining."

Clara leaned forward and took her hand. "You are doing no such thing. Merely you are stating the facts as they are, and I am grateful that you feel able to take me into your confidence. You are by no means yet on the shelf. There is time enough to catch you a husband but yes, I have to agree with you. Major Saxby is a lovely man, but you would be bored within weeks of your marriage to him. No reason, however, not to take advantage of his friendship while you may. Not in an unkindly way, you understand, but there is no doubt he is very personable, and it will do you no harm to be seen in his company. No harm at all."

"You are outrageous, Clara," Patience said, and their laughter at last drew the attention of Mary, who demanded to know what was amusing them, and the whole story had to be told again.

For some time, Patience had been troubled by her conscience. She had been in Bath for several weeks and had not yet fulfilled her promise to visit her Aunt Hester. Part of the reason for her reluctance to return was her lack of knowledge as to whether or not Lord Lacey was at home. Well, she could put it off no longer and, on a day when Clara was engaged with friends, she and Mary hired a carriage to take them to Worthington Place. It felt strange to be coming back, and Mary gazed wistfully at the gatehouse as they drove past.

Sedlescombe welcomed them and escorted the ladies to that same green salon where they had spent much of their short time at the Place.

"His lordship is away from home, ma'am. Would you like me to see if Lady Lacey is able to see you?"

There wasn't much that went on at Worthington Place that the old butler wasn't aware of, and he knew of the estrangement between Miss Worthington and his mistress. He also knew that matters had been resolved between them and that Lady Lacey had been lifted by the young lady's previous visit.

"It is her we have come to see. I hope you find her well enough to receive us but, if she is out of frame, kindly give her our best wishes and we shall go away again."

Sedlescombe could be fairly certain that they would be more than welcome but he said nothing more, merely bowing himself out of the room.

"What a peaceful room this is, Patience. Do you remember how we thought so when we were here before?"

"Certainly whoever had the decorating and dressing of it has exceptional taste."

She moved to look out of the window, but in only a few moments the butler had returned and was ready to escort them upstairs.

"My dear, I am delighted to see you. You too, Mary. It feels such a long time. No, don't explain," she added as Patience seemed about to speak. "I am certain you have had much to do in Bath and I know how quickly the days can fly when one is busy. Sit down, for you know I do not rise. I have asked Sedlescombe to arrange for tea to be brought to us, so it remains only for you to tell me what you have been up to since you left here."

"I hardly know where to begin, Aunt Hester. Mrs Buxton made us so welcome we felt immediately at home. Her husband was away on business at their country home. He still is, in fact, though I believe he is to return shortly. Their children are with him. Two boys, of five and seven, I believe," she added, knowing Hester would want to know every detail. "So Clara had sufficient leisure to indulge us, and I think we may have visited every shop in Milsom Street in her company. A delightful occupation, and one of which I think we could never weary."

"And I discovered a delightful place which stocked such a multitude of art materials that I indulged myself to a far greater extent than I should have. I have enough now to last me a lifetime, I think, for you must know that drawing and painting are my passion."

"Certainly I knew you had been sketching when at the gatehouse, Mary. Do you do portraits as well as landscapes?"

"I do. In fact, Mrs Buxton has been kind enough to invite me to produce her likeness as a surprise gift for her husband."

"What a lovely idea. Would that I could do the same, to give to my son, I mean, but I fear you are too distant to accept such a commission."

"Not at all. If you don't mind me sketching while you talk to Patience, I will be able to capture enough to work from a distance. Do you have drawing materials to hand?"

It was arranged, and in what seemed very little time Mary had committed to paper a very creditable outline of the viscountess, while Patience continued to make known to her aunt most of what had occurred during the previous few weeks. After a while she rose, and it was evident she considered it time to leave.

"You must go, mustn't you?" Lady Lacey said regretfully. "I hope very much you will be able to return soon, and perhaps you might spend a night or two here. There is so much I would still wish to talk to you about."

"We must, for we have commissioned the coachman to drive us back today, but I promise you we will not leave it so long until we call again. I'm sure I speak for Mary as well as myself when I say we should be delighted to remain a day or two with you."

"And hopefully Gideon will have returned home by then. He told me how much he enjoyed your rides together, so perhaps you might do that again," Hester said.

Patience made some non-committal reply, but her aunt's words had brought memories flooding back.

Andrew Buxton returned to Bath a week later, and Patience was privileged to see the reunion between husband and wife. They embraced unashamedly as their children clutched at their mother's skirts, keen to be included. There was no checking them, though their nurse clucked about in an attempt to control their exuberance. It was not to be.

"Now then, Dursley, I shall not have you take them away from me when they have but this moment been restored to my arms," Clara said, dismissing the nurse kindly. "Leave them with us. I shall send them to you shortly. Edward, William, have your manners deserted you while you've been away? Say how do you do to Miss Worthington and Miss Petersham."

Both performed their best bow, to the delight of the ladies and Buxton, who had extricated himself from his wife's embrace, bowed also and said how delighted he was to meet them. He thanked them, too, for entertaining his wife so well all these weeks. "And I must tell you that it enabled me to achieve far more than I had anticipated. You must know that Clara prefers Bath to the country, and I could not have left her for so long to her own devices had you not been here to bear her company."

"The pleasure has been all ours, sir. My cousin has been kind enough to introduce us into Society here, and we have unashamedly taken advantage of her goodwill."

"Nonsense. My wife is like a butterfly. She is hardly ever still and enjoys nothing more than flying from one engagement to another. That she has had you to join her will, I am certain, only have enhanced her pleasure."

"If you have finished speaking of me as though I were not here, my love, perhaps you can tell me if all is well at Buxton Manor and if you are to remain here for the foreseeable future."

She looked so fondly at her husband that Patience was put in mind of her parents, who had never been able to hide their affection from others. It also gave her pause. She had allowed the weeks to pass without giving too much thought to the future but, observing her hosts, she realised it was time for her to move on. She was as sure as she could be that Clara would protest, and just as confident that she would still see much of her cousin, even if she and Mary were to move away. The time had come to seek alternative accommodation and, while together they would be able to afford decent lodgings, they might not be in such a prestigious part of town. Well, they had been in Bath long enough to form several connections, and it was to be hoped that these would survive an apparent downgrading in her circumstances. Now was not the time to mention her plans, but she would speak to Mary and employ an agent to seek somewhere suitable for them. Meanwhile, there were two excited young boys who required diverting while their parents enjoyed their first moments together for some considerable time.

"Edward and William," Patience said, managing to engage their attention, "I must tell you that Miss Petersham is a dab hand at jackstraws and has been eagerly awaiting your return home, for your Mama tells us she can never beat you. What say you we have a game now, before Miss Dursley becomes anxious and calls you to the nursery?"

"May we, Papa?" the elder said pleadingly while William's eyes opened to such an enormous size that it would have been a hard-hearted person indeed who could say no.

"Very well, you know where to find them."

Edward ran eagerly to a sideboard in which Patience could see several other games before he pulled out the jackstraws and closed the door. This was obviously a family who were used to spending time together in childish pursuits. She fell to her knees, as did Mary, and when William looked to his parents, she suggested that they might all give them a few minutes' peace while they played together. It would have been difficult to judge who had taken most pleasure from this simple game, and it broke up only when Buxton judged it time to dismiss them to the nursery. Clara laughed as both dragged their heels and adopted the mien of poor orphans as they left the room.

"I have missed them so much, Andrew. If it hadn't been for Patience and Mary I might have run mad or, worse, felt the need to join you in the country."

Buxton looked fondly at his wife and said, "I'm afraid you must excuse me as well. My valet will be wondering what has become of me, for I promised him I would come almost immediately to change out of my travelling clothes into something more suitable for town. I will dine at home this evening. I trust you are not engaged elsewhere," he said, more in hope than expectation.

"Oh no! We are to visit the Naffertons. I'm so sorry, dearest."

"Is it not to be an informal event, Clara? Perhaps Mary and I can make your excuses?" suggested Patience.

"Would you? That is kind, indeed, and I know Lydia will understand for she is a particular friend of mine."

And so Miss Worthington and Miss Petersham went to Laura Place without their hostess, happy in the knowledge that she and her husband would enjoy their reunion. There were more than a dozen people present, one of whom was Major Saxby. Patience would have preferred it not to be so, because it had become obvious from his recent behaviour that he was once more determined to win her. She liked him. A lot. It would make her sad to lose his friendship and, try though she might to maintain a distance between them, she was unable to do so. Major Saxby was used to command and well-qualified at turning a situation to his will. Somehow, every time he saw her, he managed to separate Patience from the rest of the company. Even one or two of her new friends had commented on his marked behaviour.

On this particular evening he insisted on escorting her and Mary home and, when they arrived at the house in Upper Camden Place, she had little option but to invite him inside. Andrew was in an expansive mood and, having spent a few hours alone with his wife, was ready to welcome visitors. Unaware of the difficulty in which Patience found herself, he played the jovial host and when a particular name was mentioned, nothing more was needed for he and the major to settle down with a bottle between them discussing their time at Harrow, though they had not been contemporaries.

"Old Pershore, eh! Great science, if I remember correctly."

"Knocked me down once, and I'm not a small man by any means," Saxby said with a laugh. "I understand Jackson was more than happy to stand up with him whenever he visited his place in London."

"If you are going to talk about boxing, we will leave you to it. Goodnight, Major."

Mary had retired a while ago, and Clara paused with her cousin outside her bedchamber, biting her lip.

"That is rather unfortunate, don't you think?"

"Yes, it looks as if John Saxby and your husband are in a fair way to becoming the best of friends. How very inconvenient."

"Isn't it so?"

Clara's chuckle followed Patience to bed.

CHAPTER EIGHT

My dearest Gideon,

I hope you are enjoying your stay in London. I imagine it must be getting unbearably hot in town by now and I would hope to see you home soon when the place grows thin of company, unless of course you are off for the summer to Brighton or some such place with friends. I could only envy you if that is the case, as it grows daily more stuffy here. I spend part of each morning reading in the shade of the old oak, to which Sedlescombe is good enough to escort me, for I could not do it without his support, but I am forced indoors during the heat of the day. This year is already promising to be the hottest, in my memory at least.

My reason for writing, should you be returning to Worthington Place, is to ask that first you visit Rundell and Bridge in Ludgate Hill to collect the necklace you were kind enough to take for repair. It was one of the first pieces of jewellery your father gave me and a favourite of mine. I know I don't go out anymore but I do like to be well turned out, as you are aware.

I was delighted to receive a visit a few days ago from Patience and Mary. It seems Bath Society has scooped them up. They informed me there is barely a day when they are not engaged with friends or out shopping or acting as secondary hostesses for Mrs Buxton when she entertains visitors. I believe they will not remain with her indefinitely, for your cousin made some mention of wishing to set up her own establishment, though in a much more modest way. She has promised to come again soon and I look forward to seeing her, for she reminds me so much of her mother. Yes, I know what I said, but before all the trouble Lizzie was my dearest friend and I am focusing now on remembering the good times we had together.

Perhaps you might give me your direction if you are not planning to come home, in case there should be an occasion when I need to contact you.

Mama

Gideon read his mother's letters with mixed feelings. He had for the most part succeeded in banishing thoughts of Patience from his mind, and he'd had a fine time renewing friendships and enjoying the social whirl that London had to offer. It was possible, if one wished, to attend a ball or a soirée or the theatre such that not a single evening was be spent at home. He hadn't questioned his enthusiasm for things that he would normally have found quite tedious when taken to such extremes.

His tailor and bootmaker were both delighted with his custom, for he spent more freely than was usual. He'd purchased a new horse and was daily to be seen riding in the park. Then had come this letter, bringing with it guilty feelings for having left Lady Lacey so long and a strong desire to return home. He wondered if the promised visit would have taken place by the time he reached Somerset and felt a sudden urgency to pack up and leave immediately. Impossible, for he was committed to a card evening with Freddie Hildebrand two days hence and was dining with Adam and Oliver Conway the day after. He would not, however, undertake any more engagements, and there was a renewed buoyancy about him as he made arrangements to close the London house and prepare to leave.

"I can't say I blame you, old boy. Frankly I can't wait to leave myself. In fact, I'd be happy to join you if you can delay your departure by a week. I promised my sister I'd do the pretty by her husband's family and I've invited them to my box in Drury Lane. You're welcome to come too, if you like. In fact, I'd deem it a favour. A duller set of people you couldn't hope to find."

Gideon laughed. "I can't say that's the most appealing invitation I've ever received, but I'd be glad of your company on the journey so yes, I'll do what I can to help you entertain your guests. Didn't you say, though, that you'd only recently returned from Bath?"

"I did, but my uncle writes to say he'd like me to come again. What's a man to do, eh? As his heir, I feel constrained to oblige him. Don't get me wrong, Gideon. I'm fond of the old fellow. Beside which, it ain't like him to make demands of that sort and that sets me to worrying about him. His health isn't good. I hope he carries on for years yet, but he wasn't in too good a frame when I saw him last. In any case, with London heating up the way it is and my own folk begging me to come home, well, you've met them often enough, haven't you? Drive a man nuts, they do. I thought they'd realise by now that I'm an adult and capable of running my own life, but my poor mother wants to keep me tied to her apron strings and there's just no bearing it. And my father keeps trying to push his blunt my way, as if I were still a young buck throwing my money around. He expects me ever to be with my pockets to let."

Gideon had met the Hildebrands many times, and a nicer couple you couldn't hope to encounter, but his sympathy was with his friend. More than once he had seen Freddie acutely embarrassed by his parents' excessive anxiety.

"I have a high regard for them both, you know. They have all my life allowed me to run free about their home, treating me almost as one of their own. But I appreciate your problem. Why don't you come to Worthington Place? There could be no objection to that, and they would have no cause to be offended if you don't return home. You could visit your uncle in Bath very easily, without actually staying with him. And as you know, the city is within easy reach."

"A splendid solution, Gideon. I am now able to look forward to the prospect with no little pleasure."

On a fine July day, Gideon and Freddie set out early, wanting to cover as much ground as they could before the sun bore down unrelentingly upon their carriage. It was an uneventful journey, the latter having fallen asleep almost immediately against the cushions, having bemoaned the fact that he'd dipped too deeply the previous evening.

"You can't say I didn't warn you."

"No, but it was a dashed good wine, and it would have been foolish not to call for another bottle."

"Most of which you drank yourself."

"Which is why I consider you are to blame for the way I feel this morning. A true friend would have helped me out."

"Helped you out! You were clutching the decanter so tightly I'd have had to wrench it out of your hands!"

"Nonsense!" With which comment Freddie stretched his long legs out before him and laid a kerchief over his face to cut out the glare. Gideon smiled as it rose and fell with every breath, a gentle noise emanating from behind it. Left with his own thoughts, it was impossible not to anticipate his next meeting with Patience. She'd been in Bath for several weeks now and he had no idea as to her situation, other than his friend's mention of her being the latest craze. Deciding it was useless to torture himself, he followed his friend's example and fell asleep.

Finding accommodation proved not to be as difficult as Patience had anticipated, putting the search into the hands of an agent as she did. A very pretty house in Lansdown Crescent was not the most conveniently situated, being up a steep hill to the north-west of the city, but for two young women who had been raised in the country the five-and-twenty-minute walk from the town centre was not daunting. A measure of economy was required, and the rents in this slightly out-of-the-way area were a little more within their means. Patience signed the lease for a period of six months. It would be sufficient time for her and Mary to decide whether their future lay in Bath or, well, at this point they really had no idea what else might occur. It remained to be seen whether or not their acquaintance would feel the same way about venturing uphill, but sedan chairs were always to be had for those who could not make the climb.

It was a tearful Clara who waved them goodbye as Andrew Buxton escorted them to their new accommodation. A hug from each of the boys made Patience realise how close she had become to this family and it caused her no small pang to leave them, but it was time.

The furnishings at their new address were adequate, but she and Mary spent the next few days shopping, always a pleasure to both, for such items as would add the personal touches that make a house a home.

"I am so pleased with the colour of the drawing room," said Patience. "The pale blue walls with the only slightly darker furnishings purvey an aura of peace, don't you think?"

"Yes, this room will need only one or two additional items to make it our own."

"You have the eye of an artist, Mary. I shall be guided by you, both here and in the rest of the house. I think we've been very lucky to find something so suitable, do you not?"

"It is to be hoped our new friends will not find us too out of the way, although I suspect Simon Easton would follow you even were we to remove to Bristol."

It was true. The young man was more than ever particular in his attention, and Patience could think of no way to discourage him that wouldn't entail hurting his feelings in a way that she would consider unforgivable. In the end, salvation came from an unexpected quarter when she was paying a morning call on Mrs Sacombe.

"Miss Worthington, I should like to make known to you my granddaughter, Fanny. Her young brother has succumbed to the chicken pox, and she is come to stay with me for a few weeks to remove her from harm's way."

The girl blushed to the roots of her hair and Patience, judging her to be no more than sixteen years of age, was surprised when her grandmother announced that she was fast approaching her eighteenth birthday and a stay in Bath would be good preparation for her come-out next Season.

"You are fortunate indeed, Miss Sacombe — though I am of course sorry for your brother — that there are so many things to entertain one here. A word of warning. When you are apprised of the benefits of taking the water, I would recommend you proceed with caution. One sip was enough for me. Foul-tasting stuff, and I contrived to spill what was left in my glass so as not to be obliged to drink the whole."

It was only a mild joke, but Fanny laughed delightedly and exclaimed how clever Miss Worthington was. They talked then of the Abbey and Sydney Gardens, and Patience was prompted to invite her to join them the next day when they were to meet friends and attempt to discover the secret of the Labyrinth, "if you will trust her to my care, Mrs Sacombe, for I know you do not walk far."

The plan was greeted with excitement from the young lady and approval from her grandmother. Thus it was that Simon Easton's affections were transferred in the blink of an eye from the more sophisticated Miss Worthington to the innocent Miss Sacombe. Mindful of the responsibility she had taken upon herself in chaperoning her new friend, Patience took a great deal of care in guarding her young charge from harm, but it would in fact have been unnecessary. Mr Easton assumed the demeanour of protector and became instantly a hero in Fanny's eyes.

"How clever of you to find the way out, sir. I am sure I should have spent the whole day in the maze and never found the answer to the puzzle."

Simon would have confessed immediately that Patience had furnished him with the solution, but she caught his attention over the girl's shoulder and shook her head slightly. It seemed he had grown up fast. Instead of being in any way flustered, he merely smiled and said, "We couldn't have had that now, could we?" thus gaining Miss Worthington's approval and Miss Sacombe's further adoration.

"That was well done of you, Patience," said Major Saxby, who was walking along beside her.

"I don't believe I gave you leave to use my name, Major," she said with a slight chill in her voice.

"My apologies if I have offended you. We have become such close friends, it seems too formal for me to address you as Miss Worthington. You know of my feelings for you. I would choose rather to call you by a very different name."

She stopped so abruptly that her maid, walking close behind, almost collided with her. More exasperated than angry she said, "I had hoped we might have put this behind us. I am conscious of the honour you do me, sir, but I thought I had made it plain all those months ago when I still resided at the vicarage that I would not marry you."

"You did. You made it very plain, but I took that as being by reason of your desire to stand upon your own feet. You are an independent spirit, Miss Worthington. It is something I most admire in you, but you are now established in Bath and must have satisfied yourself as to your ability to manage your own affairs. But you are a young woman, and I desire most keenly to take those responsibilities upon my own shoulders."

"I am not yet ready to relinquish them and, forgive me, I do not harbour those feelings for you which I would consider essential in any marriage. Please do not speak of this again. And now we must walk quickly, for I have neglected my duty to Miss Sacombe and we have fallen behind."

No more was said, but from her previous experience of the major Patience could not be confident he would take her rejection this time any more seriously than he had in the past. He was a man used to getting his own way, and she felt certain that his tactics would continue as before. A military exercise in wearing the enemy down.

"Drat the man!" she exclaimed to Mary when telling her later of the afternoon's events. "If only I could find a way of transferring his affections as easily as Mr Easton's. It was a delight to see them, you know. He, of a sudden all grown up and she, well, it's nice to know her first interest has alighted on such a pleasant young man who will shield her from every passing breeze."

"Speaking of passing breezes, I am more than happy I didn't join you, once I knew you had Fanny for company. I have spent a delightful time at my easel, and my portrait of your cousin is finished. The wind has been blowing gently through the open window, and I was glad to be here rather than out in the heat of the day."

"Oh, Clara will be so pleased. Am I yet permitted to see it? You have been so shy of showing it to me."

"Not shy, but I wanted you to see it fully executed, rather than as a work in progress. Yes, of course you may see it. I am quite excited to show it to Mrs Buxton. I do so hope she will be pleased with it."

Patience was truly impressed with the finished article, instantly recognisable as its subject and portraying a hint of the humour and goodwill that encompassed who she was. "We must take it to Upper Camden Place as soon as possible. Clara cannot help but be delighted with it. Such a clever woman you are, Mary."

Mary demurred, saying that it was easy to appear clever when one enjoyed one's occupation so much, but it was evident to Patience that her friend had a very real talent.

CHAPTER NINE

"Mama, I am a villain to have left you for so long. I've brought Freddie with me, for I know you will not rake me over the coals in his presence," Gideon said, embracing his mother and genuinely contrite.

"Nor would I were he not here. You are a grown man and no longer tied to my apron strings. Don't you believe what he says, Mr Hildebrand. I am not such a poor creature, and it is a pleasure to see you again."

"In which case, Lady Lacey, why have I been reduced to Mr Hildebrand when you have been wont to call me Freddie?"

"You are right, of course. I promise not to do so again. Do you stay long in Somerset?"

"For a while, I hope. You may know that my uncle, Sir Henry Gaddesby, has received notice to quit. Hopefully not for some time, but I believe there is no cure for whatever ails him and I would not want to be backwards in showing him due respect. I expect to visit him several times while I am in the area."

"Very commendable."

"Well, between you and me, ma'am, it was as much Gideon as anyone else who has lured me away from town. He has promised me some fine sport, and the truth is that London grows thin of company and my eldest sister visits our parents at this time of the year. We don't rub along very well together, so I try to avoid her if I can."

Freddie was an ingenuous young man, and Hester took no exception at all to her home being used as a convenience. He was a not infrequent visitor and Gideon's closest friend. As such he would always be welcome.

"Now that you have paid your respects, and in my son's case reassured himself that I am well, I suggest you adjourn to your dressing rooms, for I will not sit down to dinner with you in all your dirt. Join me later, if you will. Gideon, perhaps you could have someone inform Cook that you're at home, for I eat quite sparingly when alone."

"I shall, Mama, but first I will go to the stables. I'd like to check on Thunderbolt, who should have arrived yesterday. A fine bay gelding whom I know you will admire."

"If his disposition lives up to his name, he will suit you admirably. Pass my book if you will, please, before you go. I am dying to know who the author is, for it has been published anonymously. If I wake screaming in the middle of the night I rely on you to rush to comfort me, for if ever a book was designed to give one the horrors it is this one."

"Good grief, as bad as that?"

"Worse. It's called *Frankenstein*. I shall pass it to you when I've finished, and you may judge for yourself."

"I aim to accompany Freddie into Bath tomorrow, Mama. We leave early, as he goes to see his uncle. Are there any errands you wish to charge me with?" Gideon asked on his third day back.

"If you have the time, perhaps you could call in on Mrs Langdon at 37 Milsom Street. I have ordered some lace and one or two other sundry items. It would save me the bother of arranging for a courier to bring them."

"Consider it done. We hope to return in time to dine with you but don't wait, should we be delayed. How was your necklace, by the way? Did Rundell and Bridge do a satisfactory job?"

His mother laughed. "Would you believe I haven't even looked at it? I laid the box aside when you handed me my book on the day you returned and forgot all about it. You will recall I was eager to get on with it. Look, here it is still," she said, moving one or two things on the small table beside her to reveal the jewellery case.

"Then let us examine it now." He removed the necklace and clasped it about his mother's throat. "There is no doubt my father had excellent taste, Mama. It is stunning, and emeralds suit you very well. Wear it for me at dinner tonight, if you will. It brings out the sparkle in your eyes."

"Flatterer! But yes, I will, for as you are aware it is a favourite of mine."

"My dearest Mary, it is more by far than I hoped for," Clara said with genuine excitement, gazing at Mary's portrait of her. "I am so delighted with it, but I would ask if you have any objection to me hiding it away for another two weeks. It will be Andrew's birthday, and I have an inclination to gift it to him then."

"Of course not. It is yours to do with as you wish."

They were sitting in the drawing room in Upper Camden Place, having had the portrait carried there the day after Mary had finished it. It had gone from being a drawing to a watercolour, and Mary had admirably captured her subject. In Clara's mind a plan was forming, but it was too early yet to mention. She was watching fondly as Patience sat on the floor once more playing jackstraws with the boys when the footman brought in a platter with two cards on it. She read them and raised an eyebrow before saying, "Yes, of course, Padbury, show them up." She glanced at the group of players, wondering whether to dismiss her children to the nursery but deciding instead to leave them there.

"Mrs Buxton, how kind of you to receive us. I am come to ask a favour, for I was hoping you might be able to give me the direction of…" and there Gideon stopped. His quarry, whom he had anticipated had already moved from her cousin's home, was engaged in a game with two small boys. She'd looked up when she heard his voice, her expression no less startled than he knew his own must be.

Patience was the first to recover her wits and stood immediately, smiling warmly and saying how nice it was to see him again, before having a sudden disturbing thought. "Your mother? She is well?"

"Assuredly, and sends her love. I am charged with any number of messages, all of which I have forgotten. May I make known to you my friend, Mr Frederick Hildebrand? He is at present staying with me at Worthington Place. Freddie, my cousin, Miss Worthington, her friends, Miss Petersham and —" he turned to Clara, who swiftly cleared the interested expression from her face — "our hostess, Mrs Buxton, whom I have had the pleasure of meeting a few times on previous visits to Bath. You must forgive us for barging in on you like this. We have just come from home and I had been informed — wrongly, it would seem — that my cousin had taken up residence elsewhere. I was anxious to deliver my mother's messages."

Patience laughed and the tension dissipated in an instant. "All those messages you cannot now remember. Your information is correct. Mary and I have hired a house in another part of town and are ourselves visiting. I promised the children when last I was here that I would play with them again." She turned to the boys, who were standing quietly and politely at her side. "I think perhaps we had best resume another time, don't you?"

"But you'll come again soon?" Edward pleaded.

"Certainly I shall, if only to wreak my revenge."

Edward and William left the room, the younger dragging his heels a little, and Clara rang for tea.

"Have we not met before, Mr Hildebrand?" she asked, for there was no doubt in her mind that his face was familiar.

"I did have occasion to see you in the Pump Room when last I was in Bath visiting my uncle, Sir Henry Gaddesby, but there was a crush about you and we were not then introduced. It is for that reason that I recall seeing you, for it seemed you were creating quite a stir."

"Not I, sir, but perhaps my cousin here, who had but recently arrived in the city. There were any number of people who begged for an introduction."

"Clara, you are putting me to the blush." Patience was indeed uncomfortable, for it wasn't in her character to draw attention to herself. "And here is the tea, so perhaps we might change the subject."

Freddie, though he had only just made the acquaintance of Miss Worthington, had known Lord Lacey for several years. He would have been blind not to have noticed the surprise with which they had greeted each other, but it was more than mere surprise. Something else lay beneath the surface, surely. Was his old friend hiding something from him?

"Lady Lacey told me she had received a visit from you recently and that she was vastly hoping you would repeat it soon. I am fixed there myself for some time and would consider it a pleasure to come into town and accompany you back. It is no great distance and will save you the trouble of hiring transport if you do not have your own. Worthington here has always trusted me with his carriage and horses, so I make no bones about assuming he may do so again."

"Feel free, Freddie. You always do," Gideon said with laugh. "I draw the line at Thunderbolt, though. There are other cattle in my stable who would suit you if you wish to ride."

"I for one would appreciate your escort, Mr Hildebrand," Mary said. "Lady Lacey has been kind enough to ask me to portray her likeness. It is as yet unfinished, but I would like to see her again to note some more details, over and above what I did before."

Gideon and Patience stood to one side, and he was able to say without the rest hearing, "So you have done as you intended and set up your own establishment. Are you enjoying Bath?"

"Immensely. Gideon, I was sorry not to see you before you left Worthington Place."

"You must forgive me, Patience, for removing to London without taking my leave of you. It was unforgivably rude. I have no excuse." Not one he was prepared to share with her, at any rate. "It seems from what Freddie has said that you created quite a stir the day he visited the Pump Room."

"Enough!" she said, irritated now. "I'm sure it was no more than people's curiosity at seeing someone new in their midst. Tell me, if you please, about my aunt. It has been my intention to see her again soon, so your friend's offer to escort us comes at an opportune moment. Was he correct when he said you trust him with your cattle?" Her eyes were wide and innocent, but her smile showed her appreciation.

"As it happens, yes. And while we are on the subject of horses, you heard me mention Thunderbolt, who I purchased while I was in town. I've brought him with me into Somerset. A fine specimen. I would value your opinion."

"Then it is to be hoped I find you at home when I visit your mother."

"And perhaps we could ride together again as we did before."

Gideon knew very well that he would be there when next she came to the Place. If Freddie were accompanying Patience and Mary, he would know exactly when to expect them and would make it his business to be home. In the meantime, they had fallen back into their easy manner of communication, and he could only be relieved to have it so.

He had no pretext upon which to prolong this particular visit so, having elicited his cousin's new direction and promised to visit soon, he went to fulfil his mother's request, leaving Freddie to call upon his uncle.

It was another week before Gideon was to see Patience again. Lady Lacey had contracted a severe summer cold, causing him to be tied to Worthington Place — not for reason of Hester wishing it, but because he would not leave her until her health improved. He rode in the early morning to avoid the heat of the day and to be back at home before she was awake. She did not leave her room, but he visited her as soon as he had changed his clothes and spent a while reading to her, for she was too weak even to hold a book. The doctor advised caution but saw no reason why she should not make a full recovery.

Freddie came and went as he pleased, having been bidden to treat the place as his own. On two occasions he visited Bath, and the first time he observed in the Lower Assembly Rooms that Miss Worthington had seemingly acquired a new beau. The gentleman in question was one of the city's permanent residents who had been absent for some months, travelling abroad, but who had now returned home. Mr Hildebrand, friendly as ever, toddled over to the small group to pay his respects and to renew his acquaintance with Jasper Dysart, whom he had come across once or twice in London several years ago. Simon Easton and Fanny Sacombe were there too, but they had eyes only for each other and Dysart made no secret of his interest in Patience.

Clara Buxton and Major Saxby made up the rest, and Freddie could see at once that the major was resentful of Mr Dysart. While the major did nothing unacceptable, he displayed a proprietary attitude towards Patience and his temper was in no way improved when she chose perversely to display a keen interest in what the latter was saying. Her irritation at Saxby's continuing refusal to accept rejection, though she hid it well, manifested itself in showing Mr Dysart a far greater encouragement than she would otherwise have done. His invitation to a soirée he was hosting was accepted and, though it was extended also to Mr and Mrs Buxton, she immediately regretted complying but could think of no way to retract without giving offence. Freddie, having moved away to exchange pleasantries with others of his friends, was not included in the invitation.

"I could see at once that you regretted your decision, Patience," Clara said when they were for a few moments alone together. "Is there something about Mr Dysart that you do not admire?"

"Not at all. Not something I could define, at any rate." She laughed. "I fear I have become too nice in my tastes. He is handsome, has great address and his conversation is engaging. What is there not to like?"

"And he is wealthy," Clara said with the laugh that never failed to draw a response from Patience.

"You are outrageous. Are you so determined to marry me off?"

"Yes," Clara replied, suddenly serious. "For what else will become of you? As a married lady, you could command all that Bath Society has to offer. Your life would be far more comfortable than were you to remain unwed. You are a beautiful young woman, Patience, and may have the pick of all the eligible men. Think well and choose wisely."

For the first time since she had known her, Patience found herself at odds with her cousin. "How can you say so when it is obvious to anyone how strong is the attachment between you and Andrew?" she said, again remembering her parents and her own determination to marry only for love.

"It was not always so. I was at first unsure. I don't like to sound boastful but, like you, I had many admirers as a young girl. Buxton persisted, though, and I came to see what a fine man he was."

"Major Saxby too is persistent. Would you recommend I accept his offer?" Her tone was clipped, and Clara knew she had offended her.

"Don't pull straws with me, my dear. I am thinking only of your future. And no, I cannot endorse the major's suit. He would drive you to distraction within weeks!"

The laugh was back and the tension eased, but privately Patience acknowledged the truth of what her cousin had said. Had she been blessed with a large fortune, she might have chosen to live eccentrically as she knew others had done before. Unless she wished to be shunned by Society, there was little a young woman in her position could do other than marry as advantageously as possible. The whole concept was distasteful to her, and with her usual practicality she put it to the back of her mind until such time as she might be in a better position to deal with it.

"Do you think we might visit Worthington Place again soon, my dear? Now that Clara's portrait is finished, I should like to fulfil my commitment to Lady Lacey. You know well what a perfectionist I am, and I'm at a point where I cannot proceed without seeing her again. In any case," Mary added sheepishly, "I hate to be idle and am keen to get on with it."

"I'm certain we only have to ask Mr Hildebrand to escort us, for I have no doubt his offer was genuine. I shall make it my business to apply to him the next time we meet."

That time was not long in coming, for they found him in the Pump Room when next they went.

"Will tomorrow be too soon? I plan to see my uncle today when I leave here. He seems pretty stable at present, I'm happy to say. But I have no firm plans immediately after that and would be more than happy, now that my hostess is recovered."

"She's been ill?" Patience asked, alarmed.

"Just a cold, which has kept her confined to her room. I am certain she would welcome visitors, for a more sociable lady I have yet to meet and there are times, I'm sure, when she feels starved of company."

"She did suggest that we might remain for a few days the next time we came. Do you think it forward if we pack some things to take with us? I don't need to return to Bath until Friday, when Miss Petersham and I are to attend a soirée given by Mr Dysart."

Freddie reassured her and left soon after. Upon their return to Lansdown Crescent, Patience and Mary set about immediately deciding what to take with them for a three day stay. The latter was more anxious about her art equipment for, as well as Hester's portrait, she hoped there would be opportunity for her to take her sketchbook and perhaps revisit the gatehouse. Some quick outlines would give ample material for her to enlarge upon when she returned home.

Patience, on the other hand, had ordered a new riding habit following her last conversation with Gideon. After all, the one she had was sadly worn and there was no doubt that he wished to ride with her again, given the opportunity. Had he not said as much? It had been delivered only that very day. Were she to take it with her, it might be seen as presumptuous but, if she left it behind, there was no chance she might indulge in the pastime she had so much enjoyed when staying there before. In the end, she chose to pack it with the rest. Should Gideon ask her to ride with him, she would be prepared. Should he not, well, no-one need ever know.

Patience and Mary were invited that afternoon to Upper Camden Place for tea, a quiet family affair, for today was Andrew Buxton's birthday and they knew Clara planned to present him with the portrait. Edward and William were summoned from the nursery and could barely contain their excitement for, while they didn't know what the surprise was, they were aware that there was to be one. Impossible to disguise something so obvious, but the painting had been wrapped and hidden behind a sofa until it was time. Clara made much of settling everyone in their place before retrieving it and standing in front of her husband.

"And what is this all about?" he said, feigning surprise, though she had always been in the habit of producing a gift on his special day.

"Not a word until you have opened it, sir," Clara replied, so he stood up from his armchair and removed the cloth in which it had been confined. There could be no disguising his delight. He raised the painting and turned it around, displaying it for all in the room to see.

The boys squealed their excitement. "It's Mama! It's Mama!"

Mary was no less animated. Since last she'd seen her work, it had been placed in a frame which set it off admirably. She couldn't have been more pleased, or so she thought, until Andrew walked with it over to the fireplace, removed an old family portrait and hung that of Clara in its place.

"I am happier than I can express, my dear. I would far rather look upon your likeness than that of an ancestor I never had the pleasure of meeting." He turned then to Mary, for he was aware of her hobby. "I must conclude that yours was the hand that fashioned this. I commend you on your work. It is common knowledge that drawing and painting are one of those pursuits in which young girls are educated, while boys are out learning to hunt and fish. This is above the ordinary, though. You have taken your craft to a level which, if I am not mistaken, permits favourable comparison with any whose profession it is to produce such things. Thank you."

Mary was overcome, and it was fortunate that the children chose that moment to tug at their father's arms and beg to be allowed to play jackstraws with Cousin Patience, for it gave her time to recover her composure.

CHAPTER TEN

In the morning the ladies were, to Freddie's surprise, ready when he arrived and they set off in good spirits, all three looking forward with pleasure to the next few days. He kept up a flow of small talk all the way to Worthington Place, but it was neither irritating nor shallow. He was a man of considerable intelligence which he cloaked under a veil of bonhomie, and it was doubtful that anyone in his company would ever be bored.

While Freddie's given reason for visiting Sir Henry Gaddesby so frequently was to secure his expectations, Mr Hildebrand had no need of his uncle's wealth. Fate had smiled upon him. He had fortune, was relatively good-looking, rubbed along well with everyone (except his sister) and was happy with his lot. Having spent some weeks visiting his uncle every summer as a child, he'd developed an affection for him that was almost akin to that he felt for his father. He would do everything he could to lighten the old man's last weeks but, stabilising as he had, Freddie was looking forward to a few days in the country spent in the company of Gideon, Hester Worthington, who was a great favourite of his, and two young women whose talk was not all of fashion and society. He had left his direction in the event that he needed to be summoned in a hurry but had no anticipation of that being the case. It was no wonder then that all three arrived at their destination ready to enjoy themselves.

Freddie jumped down from the driving seat to aid the ladies to step from the carriage, but Gideon was before him, having kept a keen eye on the drive for the past half an hour.

"My mother begs you join her on the terrace. On such a fine day, she chose not to be cooped up indoors."

Patience gurgled, a delightful sound. "And was it you or Mr Hildebrand who elected to bring us in an open carriage? If Lady Lacey does not object to waiting a few minutes longer, I would like an opportunity first to drag a comb through my hair which, in spite of my bonnet, seems not to have remained in place."

"Of course, though I see nothing amiss," Gideon said as he gave her his arm to lead her inside.

"How can you be so ungracious, Miss Worthington?" Freddie teased. "Had I chosen another conveyance, there would have been no opportunity for conversation."

"Mary, it would appear that the wind has been taken out of our sails. Lord Lacey, if someone would kindly show us to our rooms we will endeavour to recover our composure and join you shortly."

The bubble of laughter remained with Patience all the while, and when she and Mary stepped onto the terrace she dropped to her knees and took both of Hester's hands in her own.

"How kind of you to welcome us once more, and what a lovely day it is. So much nicer to be out here."

"And I have once more brought my sketchbook with me," added Mary. "Well, the truth is, I rarely go anywhere without it. Not to social engagements of course, or to the Pump Room and suchlike. But listen to me. I am rambling on inconsequentially."

"Not at all, Mary. It's delightful to hear you speak with such passion. Have you made much progress with your likeness of me?" asked Hester.

Mary explained that she wanted to make several drawings, each from a different angle, before deciding which would best portray her subject.

"Tell me then, both of you, how you have been finding Bath?"

There was much discussion about their new premises and of their concern that its position would prevent people from visiting them. "But it has been no such thing. We hardly have a moment to ourselves when at home, and it's been a joy participating in all the city has to offer, has it not, Patience?"

"It has indeed but, though I would not have you think me ungrateful, I have been anticipating these few days eagerly. Time to draw breath in peaceful surroundings."

"And I hope you will once more be able to ride with me while you are here, Miss Worthington," said Gideon.

He couldn't understand why she burst into laughter until she explained the dilemma with her riding habit.

"But you packed it?"

"Of course I did."

Never had three days passed so swiftly. Freddie, always happy to oblige, had on the second day accompanied Mary to the gatehouse, and he could at once perceive how she was so taken with it.

"It would be an ideal place for you to follow your hobby, would it not? I'm of the opinion that you should put it to Gideon that you reside here."

"Oh no, I couldn't do that," Mary said, flustered. "For a start, it wouldn't suit Patience and, well, I have no claim on the viscount."

Freddie believed that his friend would be perfectly happy to have the house occupied in such a way, but he could see his companion was becoming distressed so he didn't pursue the matter.

Patience and Gideon rode together happily as before, choosing to go when Hester took her daily nap. The weather was hot, but there were many wooded areas they could stick to and small rills flowed into the main stream so they were never far from water, should their mounts be in need. Thunderbolt was a magnificent creature for whom Patience had nothing but praise, a tendency to pull being kept well under control by his rider.

If the truth be told, Patience was far more at home in this environment than the round of social events she'd been experiencing of late, not that she would have admitted it to her cousin. She had made a bid for independence despite his offer to house her on his estate and nothing would prevail upon her to concede, even to herself, that she might have made a mistake. Nor, in any case, would her pride have permitted her to become his pensioner. Instead, she chose to savour every moment of her stay and daily learned more about her mother.

Lizzie had been a headstrong girl, and it was that characteristic which had landed her in so much trouble. Had she paused even for a moment to consider, things might have turned out differently. *Well, I for one am glad she did not, or I would not be here today*, Patience told herself. Was she similarly headstrong? Having decided what her fate was to be, there had been no turning her, had there? She mentally shrugged and tried to look forward to her next engagement. Had it been anything other than Jasper Dysart's soirée, she might have succeeded, but there was something about the man she could not like. When Gideon asked why she was frowning, she turned the question away, merely saying she considered it time to return to the Place, for Hester would by now be anticipating their arrival.

As they walked back to the house, the horses on a loose rein and their riders in no great hurry, Gideon expressed regret that Patience could not extend her visit. "Mama is in great spirits, and I attribute that in no small part to your presence here."

"Your mother is a wonderful hostess and makes us very welcome. Mary, I know, would love to remain longer, but I am committed to an engagement tomorrow evening and must return to Bath in the morning."

"It would seem you have settled into life in the city well. I hope it's fulfilling all your expectations," Gideon said, trying to sound sincere, for he did truly wish her happy. "I can only be pleased you managed to find time to visit us, even for a few days."

There was no irony in his voice, but his words cut her and she found her defences rising to the surface.

"You mock me, sir. You must know that it is my wish to be independent and I'm grateful indeed that Bath Society has welcomed me so, but you cannot be unaware of the pleasure I have taken this past few days. It is possible, is it not, to enjoy both town and country?"

"You misunderstand me," he answered, his own back becoming rigid. With an effort, he dropped his shoulders and lightened his tone. "I was merely complimenting you on your success. Come, let us not draw swords. Tell me, if you will, what engagement it is that pulls you away from us."

Forcing herself to relax, she told him of Dysart's invitation and was astonished to find him for a moment silent. Glancing sideways at his profile — a man had no right to be that handsome — she could see that his brow had furrowed. "Do you take exception?"

"Of course not. You are free, are you not, to go where you please? I would, however, suggest that perhaps you do not encourage that particular gentleman's friendship."

"Is there some objection? He is received everywhere and is always most amiable."

"Things are not always as they seem."

"You know something of him? Something of an unfavourable nature?"

"It is not for me to cast aspersions."

"Oh, come now," Patience said, by now thoroughly exasperated. "It is plain you disapprove and just as obvious that you have reason for your displeasure, or believe that you do. If you will not tell me what it is, then you ought not to have brought the subject up. As you say, I am free to go where I please and shall continue to do so until I have cause to do otherwise."

They rode the rest of the way in silence. All her pleasure in the past few days disappeared, and the morning could not now come fast enough for her. As for Gideon, he was deeply troubled, for there were things in Jasper Dysart's past that were damning. Things Bath Society didn't know about, but knowledge of which had come Lord Lacey's way some years ago.

In the few hours remaining, Patience and Gideon spoke to each other almost as strangers and Freddie despaired for his friend. As he drove the ladies back to Bath the next day, she asked him if he had received an invitation to the forthcoming soirée.

"I hardly know the man. Only met him once or twice, years ago. Thought he was a friend of Mrs Buxton when I saw you all together the other day."

"Then you know nothing of him?"

"Only that he's rich as Croesus and a fine-looking fellow to boot." But Patience's question had been marked enough for Freddie to make a mental note to question Gideon when he returned to Worthington Place.

Her interest piqued, Patience looked for an indication of something out of the ordinary when she attended that evening's function. She went with Clara and Andrew, Mary not having been included in the invitation and preferring in any case to remain at home. There were not above a dozen people present, and it seemed to her that their host had chosen his visitors with some forethought. All were known to her and, though his words and actions were subtle, it became apparent very quickly to Patience that she was to be singled out as the object of his attention.

On the few previous occasions that they had met, Dysart had been meticulously polite, never overstepping the mark, but making it obvious all the while that for him she was raised above the rest. He said nothing untoward, made no proprietary remarks in the manner of Major Saxby who had in such a way so irritated her. There was nothing she could have given voice to, but she could be in no doubt of the tenor which led her to believe that the evening had been arranged with her supposed wishes in mind. Every guest belonged to a small group with whom Patience had of late become most associated. Dysart had done his homework well.

The underlying disquiet she felt every time she met this man remained but, whether out of annoyance at Gideon's comments or an innate curiosity to find out for herself what lay beneath the suave surface, Patience chose not to repel. It was not in her nature to encourage any man's advances, but on this occasion she was perhaps less restrained than previously.

Dysart was clever. No-one who was not on the lookout would have been able to detect any difference in his manner towards Patience and the rest. Had he pushed, she would have retreated. Nonetheless, she couldn't but be aware of his attention, and it seemed her cousin too had been watching with interest.

As they were getting ready to leave, Clara found an opportunity to say privately, "Given your prior comments about our host, my dear, I was surprised to see you favouring him with your sunniest smile. Are you then changing your mind?"

She was dismayed. "Oh no, did it appear so? Something Lord Lacey said to me yesterday motivated me to find out more about this man. Do you..." But here they were interrupted by Buxton, who was waiting to escort them home, a sedan chair having been bespoken to take Patience to Lansdown Crescent.

"I am at home tomorrow morning, Patience. Do call on me if you are able," was all there was time for before the ladies parted company.

Patience spent an uncomfortable night running over in her mind all the exchanges that had passed between her and Dysart. Had she encouraged him? She feared that might have been the case and resolved next time they met to be more circumspect.

Sleep did not come until the early hours, and it was an unusually heavy-eyed Miss Worthington who paid a visit to Upper Camden Place. As promised, Clara was alone, having denied herself to a previous caller in the certain expectation of her cousin's arrival. Her first words were, "I strongly recommend Denmark Lotion. Nothing is more beneficial to rid oneself of unwanted shadows."

"Oh no!" cried Patience, her hands flying to her cheeks. "Is it so bad?"

"Would you prefer me to be polite, or do you want the truth? Tell me now what has occurred to upset your calm."

Patience sat with her hands in her lap but was unable to keep her fingers still, a sure sign of her agitation. "I have only myself to blame, of course. I swear, Clara, I don't think I slept a wink last night, and I am mortified that I might have put myself forward in a very unbecoming way."

Her cousin hastened to reassure her. "Certainly you did not. I would not have noticed anything amiss had it not been for our previous conversation."

"Yes, and there's the thing. It was on that occasion, you may recall, that I also perhaps showed more of a preference for Dysart than I felt. You must remember that Major Saxby was behaving in his usual way, almost as if there was an understanding between us. It was beyond bearing, and I gave more encouragement than I ought to the other. I can only hope that our friends last evening would have been unaware, but I wish now I had retained a little more distance between myself and our host."

Clara reassured her once more but was curious to know why she had behaved in such a way when it had been so evident that she had no particular liking for the man.

Patience explained, turning her annoyance upon Gideon. "It was my cousin Worthington. We were out riding during my stay, and he had enquired as to what were my immediate plans on returning to Bath. I told him of Dysart's soirée. His reaction was extraordinary. From being an amiable companion, all of a sudden he changed and became, well, I can only describe it as disapproving. And when I asked him if there was anything I ought to be made aware of, he merely tightened his lips and all he would say was that things are not always what they seem. It was obvious he was warning me, but of what? Would he tell me? He would not. My aim last night was to see if I could discover anything untoward, and that is why I behaved the way I did."

"Well, I can see how provoking Lord Lacey's comments must have been, but he can hardly be blamed for the way in which you acted upon them."

Patience crumpled. "I know," she wailed, "and that's what makes it worse."

"I suggest you go home and take to your bed, and don't go out again today unless you have to. Nothing can be gained from you showing that face in public. In the meantime, I will find out if Buxton has any knowledge. Let us meet in the Pump Room tomorrow morning to discuss this further."

Patience returned home and paused only to apply the recommended Denmark Lotion before retiring for the rest of the day.

CHAPTER ELEVEN

With her looks much improved and her mood a little more settled, Patience went with Mary to the Pump Room the next morning as instructed. One glance at Clara's face told her that her mission had been unsuccessful, for nothing was more certain than that her cousin would have been unable to conceal her excitement, had she any news to impart.

"Buxton was almost cross with me! He said he had no idea I was such a gossip, which isn't true of course, because he knows me better than anyone. And what woman doesn't enjoy a little tittle-tattle, I ask you? He said if the man had something unfortunate in his past, he had obviously left it behind him and it wasn't my business to rake it up. Well, Patience, I was as close to being annoyed with my dear husband as I have ever been."

"I do hope you didn't fall out on my account," her cousin replied, absolutely mortified.

"No, because he saw that I had tears in my eyes and was immediately stricken by remorse. Said he was sorry to have upset me and would I forgive him." Naturally Clara didn't tell Patience that she'd spent some time forgiving Andrew and that Dysart wasn't again mentioned. "Anyway, these men always stick together, don't they? I'm sure, even had he known something controversial, he wouldn't have shared it with me."

"No, I understand. The thing is … the thing is that I believe this is something out of the ordinary. I can't describe Gideon's face, but there is no doubt in my mind that he was trying to impart some sort of menace to me. Well, I doubt if I will have the opportunity of bringing up the subject again, so I suppose I must be on my guard. Oh no! Here he is now!"

"Who, Dysart?"

"No, Lord Lacey," she whispered, turning to face him. "Good morning, cousin. I had no expectation of seeing you today. Is my aunt well?"

"She is, and sends her fondest wishes. Good day, Mrs Buxton. I have come with Freddie Hildebrand."

"Who has suddenly mastered the art of invisibility?"

He laughed before becoming serious again. "No, madam, but he received news that his uncle has taken a turn for the worse. He was so distressed that I thought it best if I drove him myself. He is with Sir Henry Gaddesby as we speak."

"Oh no. My understanding is that he is very fond of his uncle and that his visits stem from affection rather than duty."

"That is true. They are, I believe, very close. By the by, I trust you had a pleasant time at the soirée you mentioned to me," Gideon said with barely a change of expression as Clara moved away. He would not tell her that accompanying his friend had not been his only reason for visiting Bath that morning, eager as he was to learn what, if anything, had transpired.

Surprised that he had raised the subject but only too aware of his scrutiny, Patience said the party had been made up of her closest acquaintance and that had naturally made for a pleasant experience. "Our host had taken every care that we should be amused. I cannot remember when an evening passed so speedily." Quickly realising that she was perhaps making too much of it and that she was in danger of prattling on, she looked at him, a question in her eyes. His own held no warmth as they returned her gaze.

"It would seem you choose to disregard my warning."

"Warning is a strong word and, until such time as you are prepared to back it up with some justification, I shall continue to form my own opinions, rather than rely on others for theirs."

"You will do as you please, naturally. I would implore you, however, to bear my words in mind. That is all I am prepared to say."

"Then I suggest we change the subject. In fact, I must return to my cousin," Patience said, moving to where Clara was talking to Mary Petersham. Gideon followed her, and she hoped he wasn't going to make the rest uncomfortable by continuing the conversation.

He did not, merely begging Mary once more to visit his mother, who had expressed a wish that she see what progress had been made with her portrait. "It was a hobby she held dear at one time, and she hadn't realised that she had allowed it to lapse. Would you believe, Miss Petersham, she has requested that her old sketchbook be retrieved from whichever trunk it had been consigned to and is to be found daily on the terrace, eagerly occupied in committing what she sees to paper."

"Of course I shall come," Mary said, absolutely delighted. "I would myself be interested to see what she has accomplished."

"Not only that, she is determined, when she has become more practised, to take up her watercolours once more. I cannot sufficiently express my gratitude, for it has made such a difference to her. Shall we say tomorrow morning, then? I will collect you myself. Good day, cousin. Mrs Buxton."

He turned away, and Patience watched as he left the Pump Room, only too aware that she hadn't been included in the invitation. She felt a constriction in her throat, and it was a brittle smile that was in place as she turned once more to her companions. There was no opportunity to discuss what had happened because they were at once surrounded by other visitors to the Pump Room, one of whom was Dysart himself.

"Good morning, ladies. Allow me to say again what a pleasure it was to entertain you the other evening. I trust you are well."

"Sadly Miss Worthington has the headache," Clara interjected before Patience was able to speak.

"Oh no. Perhaps I might fetch a glass of water. The benefits are said to be exceptional."

Patience was not proof against the impudent smile that accompanied his words. She didn't doubt that he was sympathetic but that he was equally certain she would appreciate a shared joke, for she had told him before how distasteful she'd found the waters. "You are too kind, sir, but I shall on this occasion abstain. All I require to restore me is to take a walk, and it is my intention to do just that when I leave here."

"Then I hope you will permit me to accompany you, for it is a fine day."

"And now you will believe I mentioned it for that very reason. What am I to say? Shall I be polite but decline, or shall I say thank you, that would be most enjoyable?"

She couldn't help laughing, for there was no doubting the man's charm, nor his sense of humour. She had to acknowledge also that she was in a way to being drawn in. However, Gideon's warning or no, there was still something about Jasper Dysart that she could not quite like.

Determined not to put herself in such a position again, Patience had no choice now but to accept his escort, only inviting Fanny Sacombe and Simon Easton to join them. Mrs Sacombe expressed her gratitude to Patience, saying that her legs were letting her down these days and in any case she couldn't abide walking in this heat. Privately she added, "I know Fanny is safe in your care, Miss Worthington. Mr Easton is becoming quite particular in his attentions, you know. Well, they are both young, and if nothing comes of it I am delighted that my girl's first tentative step into the world of romance is with a personable young man. But I am happy too to know that you will keep a watchful eye on them."

Patience was pleased to oblige, glad to give the couple a little more freedom which she knew they would not abuse. Mary and Clara chose to go as well and, as they were leaving the Pump Room, Major Saxby, who had just arrived and enquired as to their destination, turned on his heel to go with them.

Well, Patience thought, noticing the frown that passed swiftly over Dysart's features, *this should be interesting*. And so it proved to be. She couldn't help but be entertained by the rivalry between the two older men. Saxby couldn't hide his disapproval and became, in her opinion, more pompous than usual. His commission in the army had, she knew from her time in Oakenchurch, been purchased rather than earned. Unfortunately, in spite of being in a position of authority, he didn't have the necessary skills to accompany his rank. While he retained the title of major, he had long left the military, to which he was not suited.

Dysart, a much more polished character, would not demean himself by entering into conflict with one whom he found more irritating than challenging. He chose, in so far as he was able, to ignore the other completely. What did irk him, though, was the opportunity that was slipping through his fingers. He had envisaged an intimate walk with Miss Worthington, with perhaps just her maid to provide conformity. Now he found himself surrounded by several people whom he would not by choice have given the time of day. When they returned to the

Pump Room, where Mrs Sacombe had elected to await the return of her granddaughter, he made one last attempt, offering to escort Patience home. In this too he was foiled, Clara having previously formed the intention of taking her cousin back with her to Upper Camden Place. Jasper Dysart expressed regret, bowed and left, but there was a tightness about his lips that Patience could not like.

"I could see from your expression that our escort did not find favour with you."

"I'm afraid he did not. Not with he and Saxby spending most of the time behaving in such a manner as to spoil what ought to have been a delightful walk. You must have noticed it yourself. It would in some ways be amusing, but as I have no desire to be an object over whom men will compete, no, I did not enjoy myself."

"What a pity. I had such hopes for Dysart," Clara said, but she was laughing and that drew a laugh from her cousin also.

"Do I sound so set up in my own esteem? It was beyond bearing, truly. If it hadn't been for Fanny and Simon, I should have contrived to curtail the outing, but they were taking so much pleasure in each other's company I hadn't the heart to do so."

"You are a kind soul, Patience. Will you cut Dysart entirely?"

"No, for it would seem particularly pointed of me to do so when I have no tangible reason. Besides," she said, the ready smile apparent once more but quickly chased away by a frown, "I would find out, if I could, what is causing Lord Lacey so much alarm that he feels the need to warn me."

Patience couldn't help feeling irked when Mary waved her goodbye the next morning. Gideon had been polite but had not extended the invitation to her, merely ensuring that Miss Petersham had everything she needed to entertain and enlighten his mother. Instead, at his request, Patience went with Freddie Hildebrand to see his uncle.

"He is by no means yet out of the wood, but I've had word from his man that he has in the space of twenty-four hours shown some improvement. He would, I think, benefit from some company other than mine."

"Then I shall be happy to accompany you, and if there is anything I can do to lighten the load you have only to let me know."

"My nephew certainly knows how to cheer an old man, Miss Worthington. I am delighted to make your acquaintance, though why on earth you should be spending your time here when you might otherwise be surrounded by scores of young men, I am at a loss to know."

Patience had taken to Henry Gaddesby on sight, and nothing occurred during the time she spent with him to cause her to change her mind. He was an older version of Freddie in almost every way, and the bond between them was evident even without a word being spoken. When a sudden spasm of pain contorted his features, it was reflected in the other's eyes. This was no duty call but a display of true affection.

"I can think of nowhere I would rather be, sir. It's plain you are not a man who likes a fuss so, rather than do just that, I would ask you to tell me how I can be of service to you. I am happy to read to you but, if your hearing is unimpaired, I suggest you don't ask me to play that beautiful instrument over there or to sing to you. My skills in that department are less than mediocre and would, I fear, cause you to suffer a relapse."

The painful expression was gone, replaced immediately by a wide smile, and it set the scene for the remainder of the visit. Sir Henry expressed a desire to learn more about her. Without preamble, she told him of her recent loss and how she had moved from Oakenchurch to Worthington Place and thence to Lansdown Crescent.

"Hildebrand has told me of your connection to Lacey, but I hadn't apprehended it was so close. I've been to the Place many times in my younger days, for his father and I were friends such as Freddie and Gideon are now. Lady Lacey has always been a great favourite, and they were in the habit of entertaining on a grand scale before his demise and her own failing health. Remember me to her, if you will, when next you meet."

Patience assured him she would do just that but secretly had no confidence it would be any time soon, if recent events were anything to go by. Suddenly the old man was overcome by a fit of coughing and, though he professed when it ceased that he was quite well, she looked enquiringly at Freddie.

"Yes, yes, I can see you think you have tired me out," Henry said, intercepting the glance. "Very well, call my man if you will, but I should be delighted if you would come again to see me. I don't go out, and you have brought the sunshine into my home."

Patience took the liberty of planting a kiss on his forehead, which obviously delighted him, and she assured him she would be happy to repeat the visit.

"What a delightful old gentleman," Patience said to Freddie as they walked up the hill to her home, her maid trailing behind reluctantly, not having been country born and bred and wishing her mistress had chosen somewhere more convenient to reside. "I picture you in thirty or forty years' time. You will be just like him."

"If that proves to be the case, I shall not complain."

"It is evident that you are extremely fond of him. Have you spoken to his doctor? Are things truly desperate?"

"You wouldn't believe so to see him today, would you, but I fear he doesn't have long to live. He has recovered from this last bout, which I felt sure would carry him off, but he has proved once again that he isn't ready to leave us yet. That said, his periods of respite are becoming shorter."

"Then I would beg that you take me to see him again, for I think I don't flatter myself when I say that he enjoyed our time together."

"No question about it, and had you not offered I would have asked it of you." Freddie decided to poke his nose in where it probably wasn't wanted. "But why did you not accompany Miss Petersham today? Surely your aunt would have been as pleased to see you as my uncle was."

"I was not invited," she said simply. They had by this time reached home and she turned the conversation, thanking him for his escort and asking if she might go with him again tomorrow. "I know you will not let a day pass without seeing your uncle."

"Then I shall call for you at, shall we say, twelve o'clock?"

"There is no need. My maid will accompany me. I shall meet you there instead. Are you returning now to Worthington Place?"

"Not for a while yet. I will wait in Bath until Gideon brings Miss Petersham home, and he will take me up in his carriage."

"Then I shall look forward to seeing you tomorrow," Patience said, shaking his hand and entering the house. Suddenly, all her pleasure in the morning was gone and, with no desire to venture out again, she spent the rest of the time until Mary's return reading a novel. She didn't see Gideon, for he only escorted his passenger to the door, declining to come inside.

Patience forced a smile to her face as her friend entered the drawing room.

"I trust you found my aunt well, Mary."

"Oh yes, indeed, and so enthusiastic. First, and most important, she seems delighted at the progress I have made with her portrait, but once we got that out of the way, so to speak, she showed me all her paraphernalia. You wouldn't believe the collection she has. Some of her brushes have perished, sadly, and when she saw my watercolours in their box, she vowed to purchase something similar herself. In fact, and I was so flattered, she asked if I could procure them on her behalf. Of course, I said yes. And then, would you believe, Lord Lacey conveyed us both in his carriage to the gatehouse. You know how little she gets about, but she was determined to see what I had described to her, for she has not been there for many years." Mary paused to take a breath, not noticing in her excitement that Patience was a little subdued. "And here is the best thing of all, my dear. She invited me to come and stay, at the cottage, you understand, any time I wish and for days at a time, should I like to immerse myself in my painting. What do you think of that?" she asked with considerable emphasis.

"I could not be more pleased for you, Mary, and I'm sure I can find someone to stay with me in Lansdown Crescent during your absences."

"Oh no, I haven't made myself clear. Her wish was that you come too and spend time with her at the big house while I am busy with my work."

Patience was torn. On the one hand she would like nothing more than to spend time with Aunt Hester, and the vision of walking and riding about the estate was one that had a strong pull, but on the other it would mean seeing more of Gideon, and things between them were not comfortable at the present time. Had the invitation come from him, it would have been entirely different. As it was, she said, "It sounds delightful, to be sure, but you have not yet asked me how I spent my day. I accompanied Mr Hildebrand to see his uncle, a delightful gentleman but sadly fading, as you well know. I must tell you that he was certainly not going to allow that to get in the way of his enjoyment of our time together. I wish you could meet him, Mary. He is very much an older version of Mr Hildebrand himself. Anyway, I have committed myself to visiting him regularly and cannot withdraw from that."

"Of course you can't, but Lady Lacey and I made no firm arrangements and there is no hurry to act upon her invitation. In the meantime, I will do what I can to obtain a paintbox for her, and some new brushes, so that I have them ready when next we go."

Patience, though she said nothing to Mary, decided that it was a bridge she would cross when reached.

CHAPTER TWELVE

Patience was about to leave the house the next day when she received a call from Jasper Dysart. Noticing that she was dressed for the outdoors, he offered to escort her wherever she wished to go.

"I trust your headache is now gone, and I won't suggest again that you take the waters," he said with a smile so engaging that, had it not been for her own instincts, she would hardly have believed Lacey might know something detrimental about him. "Are you on your way to the Pump Room, or is your destination elsewhere?"

"I am on my way to see Sir Henry Gaddesby. Do you know him?"

"Some connection of Hildebrand, I believe. An old man? I cannot conceive why you should have cause to visit him," he said somewhat drily.

"Why should you indeed?" Patience said, a chill in her voice, for she considered it not to be his business whom she chose to call upon.

Dysart knew he had overstepped the mark and set about recovering ground as they walked into town. He made little progress, though he was at his most charming. The façade wavered a moment when, less than pleased to find Frederick Hildebrand waiting to take her inside, he was effectively dismissed.

"You will excuse us, I know, but my uncle is ill and is not entertaining visitors."

Dysart raised an eyebrow and looked at Patience, obviously questioning her attendance.

"Sir Henry has expressly requested Miss Worthington's company. She did much to alleviate his pain when she came yesterday."

"You were here yesterday as well?" The words were out before Dysart could prevent them, clumsy for a man normally so polished. They were not well-received and he excused himself, merely asking that she pay his respects to her host, but as he walked away it was as well Patience could not see his face. Rage was his overriding sentiment. Anger at himself that he had been betrayed into weakness. It had been a long time since Dysart had desired anyone the way he wanted her, and he was not used to being refused. Where he could not win he would take, but this was a lady of quality. She was not his for the taking. The blood burned hot in his veins.

Freddie had ridden into Bath that morning and stabled his horse while Gideon left Worthington Place and set off in quite a different direction. To the south-east of his estate at a distance of some three miles or so was the village of Combe. It was a place he visited on a regular if infrequent basis, his destination being a small cottage set a little apart from the rest. He dismounted and tied Thunderbolt's bridle to a standing post. There were a few chickens running around in the front garden, and as he opened the gate a young woman of perhaps three-and-twenty appeared at the front door.

"Lord Lacey, how lovely to see you," she exclaimed. "Look who's here, Bella," she said, drawing forward a young child who was clutching at her skirts.

"Uncle Gideon! Uncle Gideon!" the girl screeched in delight when she saw who it was, rushing towards him to be swept up in his arms.

"My word, how you have grown. Now, here is a carrot you may give to Thunderbolt while I talk to your mama," he said, putting her down and adding, "and don't forget to close the gate so the chickens don't escape. I still remember the last time I chased them up and down the lane." He entered the cottage and laid his whip on a small table, removing his gloves and casting them aside before turning to the woman, Diana. "That child is a delight. How have things been since I was last here? I can only apologise that it's been so long."

"Bella and I are both well, my lord, and I thank you every day for your generosity, for without it I dare not think where we might now be."

Gideon frowned, for he did not like to be thanked. "It's what any man would do."

"Not any man."

He looked around the room. It was comfortable. He had chosen well. "You've had no contact with anyone?"

"No-one knows where I am. You are aware that my parents disowned me when they learned I was with child, and as for that scoundrel, well, he had what he wanted, didn't he? There is no way he would acknowledge Bella, nor would I want him to. She is four years old now, and my entire focus is upon her. Even the villagers have become accustomed to having a gentry woman in their midst and treat me as one of their own. Had you not come to our rescue, we would by now be destitute. I am more than content here. I wonder still what prompted you to sponsor us, for Bella is none of yours."

He smiled a rueful smile. "I felt in some way responsible."

"What!"

"It was I, after all, who introduced you."

"Oh, come now. I was in my first season and overwhelmed by London Society. Had you not brought him to my attention,

I am certain another would have. He was determined to win me, as I found out later. Only not in the accepted way, as I also discovered to my cost. It was my parents, not you, who should have been more protective of my actions. And then, for them to cast me aside…" She brushed away an angry tear.

"He is returned to Bath."

"Dysart!"

"He has no suspicion of your whereabouts, I am certain. I established you here, as I thought that he would remain for the most part in the capital or engage in his fondness for travel. It seems now that he will remain fixed in the area for some time. I come only to advise you. I am as sure as I can be that he would not seek you out, even if he knew you to be close by. Also, I am myself no great distance away, and you know you may call upon me at any time."

Bella came bouncing into the house, and private conversation was for the time being at an end. It had been his intention to ask Diana if she might write to her parents in the hope they would by now have relented. Not that he'd anticipated an affirmative. Bitter at their rejection she had, when he had broached the subject in the past, turned it aside, and he had no reason to suppose she might have changed her mind. Still, he did not entirely despair of a reconciliation. For the time being, Diana was safe and relatively happy, but it was, in his opinion, no life for a gently nurtured girl.

Gideon rode back to Bath in a reflective mood. Why had he come to her rescue in the first place? Was it because of the tendre he had once held for her, his anger that his then friend had stolen her from him and abused her trust, or his perceived duty as a gentleman not to see her life so entirely destroyed? Perhaps a combination of the three. He had never regretted establishing her as he had, and the delight he experienced every time he met Bella was not something he would wish to forego.

His thoughts turned to Patience. There was no doubt in his mind that Dysart had set his sights on her. Because of their history, the antipathy between the two men was profound. Lacey had at first suspected that making her the object of his attention had been a way for his erstwhile friend to antagonise him. But in spite of her seeming self-assurance Patience had, in his opinion, had little experience and was not as au fait with the ways of the world as she supposed herself to be. In short, she was vulnerable. In his anxiety to protect her, he had been uncharacteristically gauche and they were now distanced from each other. Well, he may not be able to win back her affections, but he could and would keep a watchful eye on her.

There was no disregarding the worsening in Sir Henry's condition since Patience had seen him the previous day. His skin, pale before, was now ashen, and there was a strange light in his eyes. His voice when he spoke was so hushed that she had to lean in to hear what he was saying.

"A pity I didn't make your acquaintance before, my dear. I fear this is the last time I shall see you."

She took his hand and he made a feeble attempt to squeeze hers. "Your man tells us you have passed a restless night. I am sorry for that. Would you like me to talk to you? I can sit quietly by your side, if you prefer."

Gaddesby looked at his nephew on the other side of the bed. "My boy, tell this young woman that she has made my last hours more content than I could have imagined." He waved his free hand weakly and turned back to Patience. "I am happy to go, knowing Freddie has found such a friend as you. More than just a friend, I hope."

Patience was startled by the inference. Freddie too. But neither chose to disabuse the old man of what was so evidently his dying wish, and Sir Henry spoke again. "He is a good boy. Think about it." He took Freddie's hand again and pulled it with surprising vigour towards his chest, where hers still rested. He placed the one upon the other. "That's all I ask. Think about it." And with that he breathed his last, and the two were left to stare at each other across the bed, both with tear-filled eyes. They moved only when his man, who had all the while been standing in the corner of the room, watchful, patient, moved towards the bed.

"Sir, Miss, would you like me to call the doctor?" He spoke with all his usual composure, but it was plain he was much affected by his master's death.

"Yes, if you would, Burford. You have served my uncle well. Be assured you have a place in my household for as long as you wish."

"Thank you, sir, that is kind indeed. Mrs Burford and I have only been waiting... My understanding is that your uncle has left us well-provided for, and I would choose not to serve another master at my time of life, but your sentiments do you honour."

There was little more to be said, though much to be done. When they left the building, Freddie escorted Patience back to her home, his uncle's last words a barrier between them. She chose to put her friend at his ease.

"Freddie, I am more grateful than I can say for having been given the opportunity to know Sir Henry, even for such a short time. He has managed to reinforce in me how important is friendship. Please disregard what last he said. I value your companionship more than I can say, but I would not for a single moment wish you to place any significance on the words of a dying man. Do not withdraw from me out of embarrassment, for my friends are few and all are important to me, none more so than you."

She touched his arm and he placed his hand over hers. He had not, in the time he'd known her, had any thoughts of a deeper relationship. For one thing, he was convinced Gideon had a prior claim, but in these past few days he had wondered. Yes, definitely he had wondered. While the face he showed the world was one of affability and was, to some extent, superficial, it was only a cover for an intelligent and deeply thinking man. Perhaps his uncle's words had not been too presumptive after all. Without committing himself in any way, he replied, "I would never allow another man to direct my future for me. I would, however, assure you that, in the short time I've known you, you have become as prized to me as any of my other friends."

"Then I hope very much that we may continue as such. Do you return to Worthington Place today?"

"Yes, for there is little more I can do for the present, but I shall come again to Bath tomorrow, for there are arrangements to be made."

"Then perhaps you might join me in the Abbey for a short time. You may know I am the daughter of a clergyman and I go there often. I find it comforting, and it takes me away from the world to a place of peace."

Freddie was touched by her concern, and an arrangement was made for them to meet at the doors of the Abbey on the following day. It had become something of a refuge for Patience, but she was happy to share it with one who she was certain would not abuse her trust and who, in all probability, would derive solace at this particular time in much the same way as she had done.

It was a surprised Patience who greeted not Freddie but Gideon at the allotted time the next day.

"Freddie sends his apologies. He is much overcome by the death of his uncle and hadn't realised how immediate were some of the tasks confronting him. There is a wealth of correspondence which he must enter into, and this will be most easily dealt with from my desk at home."

She was pleased to see him, there being no trace of the distancing between them that had been so apparent when last they'd met. "It's kind of you to take his place."

How pleased she was to see his smile once more. "It wouldn't have done for you to be waiting and wondering where he was, and I had business in Bath. While it isn't urgent, it seemed practical to combine the two."

Patience wasn't certain that she liked the idea of being coupled with his business arrangements and looked rueful but, when he asked if something was disturbing her, she merely brushed the question aside. "And are you on your way now to such a meeting, or would you care to join me for a while? There is much to admire in the Abbey, though I make no doubt you have been many times before."

"Not for a long time. I should be delighted to accompany you and I agree, it is a most beautiful building."

While she could appreciate this sentiment, Patience wondered if her cousin was in any way affected by the spirituality of the place. For her it was paramount and a connection with her beloved father. Their eyes were drawn upwards to the fan-vaulted ceiling, which never failed to attract her attention. They parted company almost immediately, each to view on his or her own, but she glanced in his direction from time to time, noting that his interest in the memorials and architecture seemed genuine. She was certain of it when, joining her some time later, he remarked on the window commemorating the crowning of King Edgar. Experience had shown her that many came to stare only because it was a tick on their list of things to do, but it was evident from Gideon's face that he had been much impressed.

"I have been so engrossed that I've stayed longer than I ought and must be on my way. Is there somewhere I can take you before I carry out my business?"

"Thank you, no. I shall remain here a while longer. Do please offer my condolences to Mr Hildebrand. Yesterday seems so unreal that I am not certain I did so then."

"I will be sure to carry your message to him. I believe Miss Petersham is planning on visiting my mother again soon and staying for a while at the gatehouse. It would give me great pleasure if you could join her, if your commitments are not too taxing. I enjoyed our rides together when you stayed before and would delight in repeating the experience."

"You are very kind. I will discuss the arrangements with Mary and let you know when to expect us. I look forward to seeing Aunt Hester again —" a broad smile spread over her face — "and to admiring what progress she has made with her own artwork."

Gideon grinned. "You may laugh, but I can assure you Mama has sufficient expertise to impress. Well, she impresses me at least. Very well then, if not before, I look forward to seeing you soon at Worthington Place."

He left and Patience sat in one of the pews, intending to meditate for a while, but her thoughts kept drifting back to her cousin. Were they going to be on good terms again after all?

CHAPTER THIRTEEN

It was almost a week before Patience and Mary were able to discharge all of their commitments and leave Bath. Mary had become something of a celebrity on account of her portrait of Clara Buxton. From its prominent position over the fireplace, it had attracted much interest and no little admiration and, upon being asked who the artist was, its subject had had no hesitation in putting Miss Petersham forward. As a consequence, she had been commissioned to portray several images. Embarrassed at first, though naturally delighted, she was grateful for the opportunity to practise her skill. Had it not been for Clara, however, her efforts would have remained financially unrewarding.

"I couldn't possibly," Mary had protested when encouraged by Mrs Buxton to set a price for her work.

"How could you not? Try for a moment to reverse the roles. Would you, in Mrs Sacombe's position for instance, be comfortable asking someone to invest so much time without recompense?"

There was no arguing with Clara's logic, and with the list of potential customers growing daily Mary felt a real need for a proper studio. She said as much to Hester when she and Patience finally arrived at Worthington Place and had been there sufficiently long to have settled down to a nice catch-up.

"But surely the gatehouse is laid out in such a way as to provide such an opportunity," said Hester.

"Indeed it is, but I cannot be travelling from Bath every day. I'm sure I shall manage in Lansdown Crescent, even though the light is less beneficial there."

Patience shifted uncomfortably in her chair, aware that in keeping Mary at her side she was preventing her from fulfilling a dream. Before any more could be said, Gideon entered the room with Freddie in his wake. Patience rose immediately, happy to turn from a subject to which she had as yet no satisfactory solution.

"You see us at last, gentlemen. When you issued your invitation, sir, I had not calculated how long it would take Mary and me to fulfil our immediate obligations. I cannot tell you what a relief it is to know that for the next few days at least I will not be pulled this way and that and may do exactly as I please."

Gideon laughed. "I see you have not yet had sufficient conversation with my mother. I am certain she has every moment of your stay mapped out for you."

"Don't be ridiculous, boy, it's no such thing. Just one or two ideas I have had for your entertainment, Patience."

"Your son delights in teasing me, I know. I shall take no notice." Patience couldn't help reflecting upon how comfortable she was with these people whose sense of humour so matched her own. *I must not let it weaken my resolve, for I make no doubt my cousin would renew his efforts to persuade me to stay should he perceive the smallest chink in my armour, particularly in the light of Mary's requirements*, she thought. She turned to his friend. "Freddie, I have had no opportunity to properly offer you my condolences. Everything happened so quickly when last we met, and I thank you again for allowing me to share those last moments with your uncle. In those two days, I became fonder of him than I can say."

"It is I who must thank you, Patience, for I have no doubt at all that you made his passing so much kinder than it might otherwise have been."

"Then we were both blessed. Is there much still for you to do?"

"No, for I have passed things into the hands of my agent, who will consult me when necessary. There will be the reading of the will, of course, but I expect no surprises there. In fact, I should prefer it if he has left his fortune to an orphanage or some such thing. I have no need of it, and I am aware that there are those who have misconstrued my attentions towards him in the past, believing me to be ingratiating myself for my own ends." Freddie shrugged his shoulders in a fatalistic manner, but it was evident he was much affected.

It was Mary who broke the silence that followed. "What nonsense. No-one who has heard you speak of him could have doubted your genuine affection for your uncle. Will you remain fixed in the area after the funeral?"

"If Lady Lacey is not too put out by my continued presence, I shall stay awhile. I should not choose to be in London at this time of the year and, if my mother's letters are to be believed, my sister shows no sign of removing herself from our place in Hertfordshire. You may recall me saying that she and I have a tendency to come to blows if required to spend more than a few hours in each other's company."

Hester made it plain that their visitor might continue at Worthington Place for as long as he wished. "There is no doubt that the conversation at dinner is more enlivened by your presence."

"Well, I thank you for that, Mama," said her indignant son.

"And speaking of dinner," she continued, only a smile acknowledging Gideon's comment, "I would suggest that we adjourn now and give the ladies an opportunity to settle in at the gatehouse. But do come back later, won't you, and join us."

She had turned to Patience and Mary, who had once more risen at her words.

"I know I speak for both of us when I say we shall be delighted to do so. Come, Mary, our things have been deposited already and it is a fine afternoon for a walk."

Gideon and Freddie both insisted on escorting them to the cottage, and it was with the anticipation of an exceedingly pleasant interlude that they parted company.

The next few days proved to be as enjoyable as everyone present had foreseen. Patience and Gideon resumed their daily rides and succeeded in not falling out once. Sometimes Freddie joined them, and on other occasions he would take out a fishing rod or a gun, or tenderly escort his hostess to the gatehouse where she delighted in watching Mary at work. Under such propitious conditions the portrait of the viscountess was completed and required only to dry completely before a suitable frame might be found to set it off at even greater advantage.

"Such vanity. And now I don't know where to hang it, Mary, for I'm sure I have no wish to see my own likeness every time I enter a room. On the other hand, I am sufficiently proud to wish visitors to observe the skill with which you have discharged your commission."

"You cannot conceive of how delighted I am, Hester, but it is after all only a watercolour. I should wish in the future, if you have no objection, to attempt your likeness in oils. It is a medium in which I am not as practised but one I enjoy, and I would welcome the opportunity to improve my aptitude."

Patience wasn't present at this conversation or any of the similar exchanges between the two, but she couldn't be unaware of the glow that was so apparent in her friend or the pleasure Mary and Hester took in each other's company, despite the dissimilarity in their ages. With sufficient interest in her work to suggest she might earn more than enough to support herself, it would be cruel indeed if Patience kept her friend indefinitely by her side. This placed her in a severe predicament. She could not — would not — accept her cousin's charity. She must instead find another to bear her company in Lansdown Crescent. At the end of the week it was with mixed feelings that both Patience and Mary returned to Bath, the former to find a note awaiting her from her cousin Clara.

My dearest Patience,

I trust you had a fine time at Worthington Place, although I cannot but be glad that you are now returned to Bath (which you must now be if you are reading this). Can you believe that William has broken his arm! My heart broke, for I was with him when it happened. Just a foolish accident, but his cries of anguish touched me deeply. Andrew has a full schedule of commitments and must remain in town, but we are both of us convinced that our boy will do better at Buxton Manor. I have waited only until your return and would beg you come to see me as soon as you are able.

Clara

It being still early afternoon, Patience went immediately to Upper Camden Place, only to find her quarry was out but expected to return shortly. She used the intervening time to visit the nursery, where Edward was in fine fettle but his younger brother was looking rather pale and, though he was obviously pleased to see her, he did not display his habitual excitement.

"Your mama has been telling me in a letter she wrote that you have been a brave warrior indeed. Did you slay your dragon before being yourself incapacitated?"

"It wasn't knights and dragons. We were playing chase, and it was all Edward's fault. He moved a stool and I tripped over it. Papa said I wasn't looking where I was going, but I was. Well, most of the time. And then he said we shouldn't have been running around the furniture. Papa, that is, not Edward."

"I'm sure your brother didn't mean to trip you up, did you, Edward?"

"No, and in any case, how was I to know he would break his arm?" came the somewhat contradictory reply.

"Well, it seems from her note that your mama means to take you to Buxton Manor, where I am certain you will have more room to run about when you are once more able to do so, William. Do you leave soon, do you know?"

"The accident happened two days since, but I know Mama was waiting for you to return to Bath. Nurse said she will hold me very tightly so I am not jolted in the carriage. It really hurt, Cousin Patience," the little lad said, biting his lip manfully to stop the tears.

"I'm sure it must have done, and I can only marvel at your courage. You will in time slay many dragons, but first you must give your arm sufficient time to heal. I have no doubt your mama is wise to take you into the country in the meantime."

"And will you come with us? I know Mama is hoping so."

Patience had no time to react to this news, as Clara entered the room just as her son was letting the cat out of the bag.

"Thank you, William. I had hoped for a more gentle approach to my request, but I see you are before me. Not that it isn't so, cousin, for I should dearly like you to accompany us. But let us leave these two ragamuffins here and adjourn to the drawing room, where we may discuss the matter in more comfort and away from ears that hear things they oughtn't to and repeat things they shouldn't," Clara said, somehow managing to glare at and laugh with her children at one and the same time.

Once they were alone, Clara explained the request. "I'm so sorry I wasn't here when you arrived, Patience, and even more so because I would much have preferred that you learned of my plan from me, not the children." She offered her visitor a cake to accompany the tea which had been brought in by the footman. "It is true, though. I would dearly like you to join me if you can. As I told you in my note, Andrew must remain in Bath. I have mentioned previously that I do not myself do well in the country, but for the sake of my children I must go." She tried to look the martyr but succeeded only in giggling. "Well, no-one is fonder of her sons than I, but a prolonged period at Buxton Manor without my dear husband is not what I would choose. I shall be bored within a sennight. And that's when I thought of you. Not to come for several weeks, of course. I could not ask that of you. But for a while, if you can."

Patience could not withstand the plea in her cousin's eyes and she was in any event conscious of the debt of gratitude she owed her. "I am committed tomorrow evening but will cancel everything after then. I could travel on Thursday if you can wait, or follow you if you need to go sooner."

"Two days more will make little difference, and it will give William a little more time to build himself up for the journey. I shall make the arrangements then, if you agree," Clara said hopefully.

Patience had been thinking all the while and responded with assurance. "Mary will, I know, be happy to return to Worthington Place while I am gone. As it was, I had to drag her away, and there is a standing invitation for her to visit at any time. I should be delighted to come with you, Clara."

She saw the strain vanish from her cousin's eyes and left soon after to break the news to Mary.

As luck would have it, Gideon and Freddie rode into town together the following day and, having stabled their horses, headed straight for the Pump Room where they hoped to meet Patience and Mary. Gideon's errand (he said) was to assure the latter that he would be happy to transfer any materials to the gatehouse at her convenience. "You must know that my mother is a changed woman on account of you," he told Mary. "She asks me to tell you that she would be proud to sponsor you so that you may carry on your work."

Mary was hugely embarrassed. "No, no, indeed, that shouldn't be necessary, grateful as I am. People have been so kind, and I have so much work commissioned that I hope to be able to support myself, if not immediately then perhaps in the not too distant future."

"Would you at least agree to maintain a studio at Worthington Place for such times as it might be convenient for you to work there? I cannot tell you what a difference it has made to the viscountess and to what extent her enthusiasm seems to have overcome some of her pain. Or, at least, she is prepared to suffer it in pursuit of her interest. She made not a single complaint when going to and from the cottage during your recent visit."

He cast a quick glance at Patience, aware that he needed to tread carefully. He would have been more at ease had he known his cousin had already accepted this seemingly inevitable outcome and that she had only relegated it to the back of her mind because of her impending visit to

131

Malmesbury. It was Clara, arriving at that moment, who informed the two gentlemen of their plans.

"Lord Lacey. Mr Hildebrand. How delightful to see you in town. I fear I must make the most of this opportunity, for Patience and I are about to leave Bath for some weeks. My youngest has had the misfortune to break his arm and Buxton wants me to remove him to the safety of the country. Though with the damage already done, I don't quite follow his reasoning. However, there will be more for William to do there, I dare say. Unfortunately my husband is fixed in Upper Camden Place for some time, so I have begged Patience to accompany me." She rattled on in this vein for a short time until Freddie managed to intercede to enquire when they were to leave.

"We go tomorrow. It is only some prior commitment of Miss Worthington's that keeps us until then. But wait. I have an idea. It is not so far to Buxton Manor, after all. Perhaps you might find time to visit us for a few days. We can offer you plenty of sport, and our trout stream is second to none."

Few could resist Clara when she was at her most engaging and both promised they would be honoured, if it wouldn't put her to too much trouble.

The giggle, spontaneous as it was, left them in no doubt that she would be delighted to see them.

"Do you go as well, Miss Petersham?"

A flush covered Mary's face, but she didn't hesitate. "I do not, sir, and in the light of your mother's kind offer I was wondering if I might perhaps return to Worthington Place while Patience is away."

"Not only that but I shall come and collect you myself. Will I require an extra carriage to convey your materials?" Gideon said with a laugh.

He was a little taken aback when Mary replied impishly, "I don't *think* so. I shall make it my business, however, to go shopping this afternoon, for there are many things I require and a few which I promised Lady Lacey I would procure for her. I thank you for the offer and will make sure to be ready for your arrival tomorrow."

It seemed that for the time being things were working out satisfactorily. Patience felt a pang, acknowledging only to herself that her preference would have been to go to Worthington Place rather than Buxton Manor. She berated herself for being a selfish creature and put the thought aside, remembering instead how much she enjoyed the company of Edward and William, as well as that of their mother, and that she could safely look forward to a visit from both Gideon and Freddie during her stay.

Patience went that evening to a select party which Mrs Sacombe was holding for her granddaughter. There were perhaps some twelve people who sat down to supper, and she knew her invitation had been given in order for her to act as a link between the generations.

"I know I can rely on you, my dear, and my hearing is none too good these days. I hope you do not take offence when I say that I ask you to stand as assistant hostess, at ease as you are in all company."

"On the contrary, Mrs Sacombe, I am flattered by your trust in me and will do what I can to help."

There were two of the old lady's widowed friends to bear her company and half a dozen young people. She was delighted to see that Simon Easton was of their number. For the rest, well, it wasn't her party and she had no say in who would be attending. She would have preferred the number had not been made up by Jasper Dysart and Major Saxby and could only assume that Mrs Sacombe had believed she was providing suitable entertainment for her.

The major behaved with all his usual condescension but inevitably became very stiff in his conversation with Dysart. The latter wasted no opportunity in goading his supposed rival but Patience, however irked she might be with her suitor's postulating, could not admire these tactics which served, as intended, to bring out all that was most foolish in the man. It was unkind and unnecessary, and she took no pleasure in seeing another used for sport. When Dysart, in a quiet moment, had the opportunity for some private conversation with Patience, she reprimanded him soundly.

"It is not for you, sir, to dictate another's behaviour. I wish you will not tease him so, for I fear it only highlights your own deficiency as well as his."

He was taken aback. The words had been spoken with a smile, but there was no denying the rebuke behind them. For a moment he hesitated but recovered quickly, saying, "Then I apologise wholeheartedly. I had assumed, perhaps erroneously, that his attentions were not welcome to you and was endeavouring in my evidently clumsy way to relieve you of his company."

"I am perfectly able to snub any unwanted approaches without your aid or indeed anyone else's. You would do well to remember that, sir."

He bowed slightly, accepting the reproach, but inwardly he was suffering from contrasting emotions. On the one hand he was seething. He did not like to be caught off balance. On the other his blood was boiling in quite a different way. He thought Patience magnificent, and he wanted her like the devil. As with all good campaigners, he took stock of the situation and for the moment withdrew, knowing that to continue would only add fuel to her flames. While he was certain this would be spectacular to see, it would in no way advance his cause. He spoke only once again to her during the evening but planned to call on her on the morrow, armed with a posy and a smile and a determination to recover ground. Unfortunately for Jasper Dysart, by the time he reached Lansdown Crescent his quarry had flown.

Patience had been very careful to make no mention the previous evening of her intention to leave Bath and, as no-one else present had been aware of her plans, she was able to go, secure in the knowledge that neither of her unwelcome suitors would know of her whereabouts. All other avenues having led to a dead end, it would be many days before Dysart paid a visit to the Buxtons' home in Upper Camden Place to see if he could ascertain Miss Worthington's present location.

CHAPTER FOURTEEN

Patience didn't see Gideon on the day of her departure, having left Lansdown Crescent before he arrived to collect Mary. She, in a state of high excitement, had told her friend, "I do hope he will bring a large carriage, my dear. Though we joked about it, I fear not everything will fit. I believe I exceeded Hester's wishes. Those items I have purchased for her, combined with my own, will take up more than the available space if he brings only a curricle."

Patience had laughed. "I suspect after what you said that he will ensure there is sufficient room for any luggage. And I must leave you now, or I fear my own carriage will go without me. I promised Clara we might leave promptly."

Clara and Patience arrived at Buxton Manor towards mid-afternoon, the sun not yet having dipped in the sky. Edward and William had become restless during the last hour or so and their fond mama was finding it hard to maintain her calm and to keep them occupied. In this she was ably assisted by her cousin, who devised a game whereby the first to spot a designated tree or a bird of some species or another would be accredited with a tick, the first to accumulate ten being the winner. Fortunately for the peace of all, neither boy reached the target before they arrived at their destination and, free from the confines of the carriage, they once more became their good-natured selves. Nurse Dursley bore them off with promises of lemonade and Clara, removing her bonnet and behoving Patience to do the same, sank into a chair and declared she had never been happier to be home.

"It is beyond me how you managed to maintain your calm with my children jumping around, their voices so shrill that I thought my head would burst."

"Nonsense. You were just as engaged in their entertainment as I. It was good to see William entirely unaffected by the restraints of the sling that was supporting his arm. I must say, Clara, I think you did right bringing them into the country. He will do far better here than in Bath, where there are fewer opportunities for him to work off some of his boundless energy."

"I believe you are right, and your ingenuity on the journey has inspired me to devise a treasure hunt in the grounds. Both boys were so engaged that I do believe we could keep them healthily and happily occupied for hours. I shall consult with the gardener, for we don't want something too taxing for William, encumbered as he is by his arm, or too boring for Edward so as not to be a challenge."

In spite of Clara's previous protestations, it was evident that she loved her country home. It was an imposing house and, though not overly large, sufficiently so to accommodate several guests in the numerous bedchambers. The one allocated to Patience, greatly to her liking, had been decorated and fitted out with blue hangings, its window facing the morning sun and overlooking well-manicured gardens to the rear of the house. Beyond was open country which she hoped to explore, her cousin having said earlier in the day, "Though I am not fond of the sport myself, I know you love to ride. I am sure there will be a suitable horse in Buxton's stable, and you are welcome at any time to take my groom with you if you wish to venture out."

They were enjoying a quiet supper together later that evening when Patience commented, "You profess not to like living in the country, yet there can be no doubt that you are fond of this place and that yours has been the hand that has made it so comfortable and welcoming, for I recognise your touch from Bath."

"You are right, of course, but you will find that in no time at all I shall become impatient. I do not have your love of the outdoors and must forever be surrounding myself with people, not being one of those who is content with their own company. It is why I so much wanted you to come with me." She laughed, the tinkling sound that Patience had grown to like so much. "You will soon become acquainted with all my neighbours. I could not, in Andrew's absence, have entertained as I would wish on my own, but with you to act as second hostess there can be no objection. Did you think you had come to withdraw from company for an extended period? It will be quite the reverse. I can only hope that between organising house parties and ensuring the boys are sufficiently occupied, you will not be running back to town sooner than anticipated."

"You need not fear. I am more robust than I appear. Do you have any immediate plans, for tomorrow, I mean?"

"I must consult with the housekeeper. It is a while since I was last home and I know there will be a number of things she will wish to discuss with me. A bore but a necessity." Patience wasn't convinced by Clara's protestations. There was a housewifely side to her that she liked to keep hidden. "You might if you choose visit the stables. Jackson will be more than happy, I know, to introduce you to every beast we have and to discover what may be your skills so as to allocate a suitable mount for you."

"Actually, if Nurse has no pressing schoolroom tasks for them, I should like the boys to show me around the grounds if you have no objection. It will be a release for their energy after spending the best part of today cooped up in a carriage, and I will enjoy seeing things through their eyes."

"I knew I was right in asking you to come with me," Clara said triumphantly.

Patience was to find soon enough that her cousin was as good as her word. By the third day following their arrival, the first guests arrived. It was only a small affair. Dinner for eight, those present being long-standing friends of their hostess. All the latest gossip was caught up with, Clara delighted to learn that the Squire Mulberry's daughter had recently become engaged to a young man she had known from childhood.

"I saw no notice in the papers," she exclaimed, for it was her habit to follow social announcements, being interested in all, whether they be births, marriages or, sadly, deaths.

"The reason being, my dear, that it is to appear tomorrow," said Mrs Mulberry with a laugh, obviously delighted with the forthcoming nuptials of her eldest, having three more young ladies to dispose of.

They had brought with them their son, a young man of some twenty-eight summers, the eldest of their progeny and of whom they were inordinately proud. Thomas had fought at Waterloo and returned home a hero. Of quite a different cut to Major Saxby, he exuded a quiet air of authority and Clara had invited him expressly with the intention of introducing him to Patience. They had got along famously and almost the first thing they did was to arrange to go riding the next day. Mrs Buxton was pleased, for she desired nothing more than to see her young relative established in the world. She was not to know that each had, in the other, found a friend with similar interests and a comparable sense of humour. That there was not a spark of romance between them she was not to learn for some days, so she continued to live in hope.

Invitations were reciprocated and others received, and in no time it seemed the whirl of activity was as great, if not more so, as it had been in Bath. There was no doubt in her mind that Patience preferred this way of life to one in the city and even Clara's sentiments were changed, so busy was she. That she missed her husband there could be no doubt. They were unfashionably fond of one another, and she was delighted when he returned home. "But I am only here for two days, my dearest, as I still have business in town to which I must attend," he said with regret. "You will forgive me when I tell you I could not bear being parted from you for so long and can only be grateful that the proximity of Buxton Manor makes it possible for me to come back frequently and with little inconvenience."

Of course she forgave him and, had it not been for Patience, she might have been tempted to leave the children with their nurse and go with him to Bath. However, common sense and maternal feelings compelled her to put aside her own wishes, and it was only the prospect of a picnic on the day following Andrew's departure that enabled Clara to act with circumspection.

Three days later Jasper Dysart arrived, full of apology for his intrusion but informing his hostess that her husband, whom he had called upon the previous day, had assured him he would be welcome. Wishing him elsewhere, she had no alternative but to invite him to stay. It would have been hard to establish who was more vexed when Patience and Clara discussed it later. "He is just the sort of man who will outstay his welcome," said Patience.

"What welcome," Clara laughed, though she was rueful, "when neither of us wishes for his company? It isn't even as though Buxton is here to take him shooting or divert him with whatever else gentlemen get up to when we females are not around."

"Perhaps we might enlist the help of Thomas. I have no doubt he will appreciate the predicament in which we find ourselves."

Clara had by this time realised that while Patience and Thomas were not destined for the altar, they had become firm friends. "An excellent idea. He may even find a way of getting rid of him."

"Not he. I fear Dysart is like a burr which adheres to one's clothing and is so difficult to remove."

"Well, Thomas is a campaigner, so we must put our hope in him."

Patience had no hesitation in asking for Thomas's help for they had, in just a few short days, established the intimacy of old friends, each secure in the knowledge that any secret would be safe with the other.

"He is immune to polite rebuffs, Thomas. While this wasn't a problem in Bath when I saw him infrequently and only with other people, imagine how difficult it will be with him staying in the same house. Just listen to me! I sound so puffed up in my own esteem, you must think badly of me."

"Not at all. I've met his type before and will do everything I can to shield you from him."

"I fear he will engage to join us on our morning rides. He brought his own horse, his luggage following in a carriage with his valet. The effrontery of the man, so sure was he of his reception."

Thomas smiled in sympathy. "He cannot be blamed for that if Andrew assured him of his welcome as he has suggested."

"I shall have a word or two to say to Andrew when I see him again."

The smile became a grin. "You would tell him who to welcome into his own home?"

"What am I saying? The man has driven me distracted. And look, we are nearly returned to Buxton Manor. Do not desert me, my friend, for I fear this will be our last opportunity to enjoy our comfortable rides as before."

"You may be assured of my presence here tomorrow as usual, though I fear our confidences must be at an end for some time."

Thomas was as good as his word, but he couldn't be with Patience every moment of every day and it was inevitable that Dysart would find a way to separate her from Clara.

Jasper Dysart was exercising caution. No fool, he realised he had offended Patience when last they'd met and he exerted himself to be as charming as he knew how, and no-one could be more so than he when he wanted. He couldn't feel he'd made any immediate progress, but he was content to bide his time. His hostess had arranged many activities and, through his meetings with her guests, he contrived to be invited to most that she and Patience were to attend. Handsome, wealthy and of considerable address, he was seen to be an asset to any party. When at Buxton Manor during the day, he was at leisure to make what he could of his position as the only gentleman in the house.

Patience spent much time with the children, something which gave her a deal of pleasure as well as a separation from her suitor. She was still unable to understand what it was about him that repelled her and not once did he overstep the mark, but she could never feel entirely at ease with him. And still he waited. He realised soon enough that her daily rides were always accompanied by Thomas Mulberry, and instead of persisting in joining them he used the time to charm his hostess, hoping it might serve him well in the future. Clara, no green girl, could see through him as easily as a pane of glass in the mullioned windows of her house. She was content to humour him, for there was no doubting he was excellent company, but fooled she was not. Dysart had, however, severely offended one of his recent acquaintances. On the fifth day of his visit, Patience and Thomas were again riding together when she asked him why he had a fixed frown on his face.

"It does not suit you, sir, and makes me believe that you are not enjoying my company."

Thomas didn't come back with any pleasantry but instead reined in.

Patience followed suit, now genuinely concerned. "What is it, Thomas?"

"I should like to know why that man is conducting what I consider to be inappropriate behaviour towards my sister Emily. She is barely seventeen years old and no match for one of his experience."

"Oh no! When has he had the opportunity to do so?"

"I thought I was imagining it at first, just little things when we were in company. Nothing I could call him out on but, well, you know. And then I find that for the past two days, when you and I have been riding, he has called upon my parents and begged to escort Emily around the garden. Naturally her maid was only a few paces behind, but…"

"Yes, he is far too old and accomplished for her. An innocent wouldn't have the experience to turn aside the type of flattery I suspect you have in mind. Have you talked to your parents of this?"

He said that he had not. He was reluctant to distress them and, for all his habit of command, he was at a loss as to what to do.

"Tell them of your concern. That you think perhaps one of your other sisters should also accompany them. Squire and Mrs Mulberry, for all their position in the community, are not I think acquainted with men of Dysart's stamp and may not have noticed anything untoward. I wish you would speak to them, for I feel in some way responsible. Not to put too fine a point on it, you are aware that I believe he has pursued me into Wiltshire. Perhaps, forgive me, having seen that his tactics are not working he has turned to easier prey."

"It is a possibility."

"Come, let us return at once. I must tell Clara and see if we cannot devise a way to be rid of the man."

Patience was more distressed than she could say, but in the end the problem was resolved not through any machinations of hers but due to the arrival at Buxton Manor of their host, Lord Lacey and Mr Hildebrand.

The men had all three ridden together, Andrew using Gideon and Freddie as an excuse to steal another two days from his busy schedule. He would spend the whole of the next day at home before once more returning to Bath. The other two were to remain at least until Andrew's next visit. "Clara prefers town to country, and I am relying on you to keep her entertained in my absence," he informed his companions.

"Happy to assist, old boy, and with my uncle's funeral behind me and not being any longer obliged to maintain a watchful eye on him, I feel as if my life is once more ordered," said Freddie. "Not that I begrudged a moment spent with him, you understand. Fond of the old man, I was. What are you laughing at, Gideon?"

"The thought of your life being ordered, Freddie, what else? I have never met a man more disorganised."

"No, how can you say so? Andrew, you'll bear me out, won't you?"

"I'm afraid not, old chap. I fear Lacey is correct."

They had by now reached Buxton Manor, climbed the steps into the house and were laughing, all three, as Dysart emerged from the drawing room to encounter them with a shocked expression on his face. No more so than the viscount and Mr Hildebrand, Andrew having omitted to inform them that he was there, having on the one hand forgotten and on the other being unaware of any animosity between the parties concerned.

Joviality turned to formality as greetings were exchanged and the newcomers entered the room that the other had just vacated, leaving him to continue on his way upstairs, glancing briefly over his shoulder and displaying a scowl, though there was none to see. Inside the room the atmosphere was entirely different.

"Papa, Papa, you are come home again."

"I am, William. Yes, Edward, a very creditable bow. Now, if you will but calm yourselves a moment I will have an opportunity to greet Mama and Miss Worthington, and perhaps Lord Lacey and Mr Hildebrand will forgive your exuberance."

Decorum was never much in evidence in the Buxton household and the boys' mother made no attempt to suppress their high spirits, especially as they were encouraged outrageously by the new arrivals.

"You have just missed Mr Dysart, gentlemen. He had reason to go to his room for something," Clara said with a twinkle because she well knew how he would be accepted by these two, having witnessed previous exchanges between them. "But he will join us later when we dine, so you will then have an opportunity to renew your acquaintance with him."

Neither responded, Gideon adroitly turning the subject by commending William on his progress and asking if he was sufficiently dextrous to play jackstraws with his uninjured arm. Patience joined her cousin in teasing the boys, feeling all at once as if a weight had been lifted from her shoulders.

CHAPTER FIFTEEN

Dinner that evening was a strange affair. With only six sitting at the table, it was impossible for Lacey and Dysart to conceal the tension between them, though neither said a word out of place. Patience could only conclude that whatever Gideon had tried so ineptly to warn her of was not merely a resentment against the other. Something grievous had occurred, that much was obvious.

Clara, delighted to have her husband home, chatted on in her usual enthusiastic manner, but even she could not be unaware of the undercurrent. Freddie had long known how things were between the two men, though he had no knowledge of the cause. He did his best, engaging Patience in conversation.

"I must thank you again for your kindness during those last hours of my uncle's life. Now he is laid to rest, I can at least console myself with the certainty that his passing was neither painful nor lonely, and that you gave him much solace."

"I feel honoured to have met him. A lovely gentleman, and one who will long remain in my memory. I only wish our acquaintance could have been of longer duration."

"I understand, but he would not have wished to linger as his condition worsened, and I will be forever grateful that he had even those two days with you."

"Then I am content. Do you now leave Bath?"

"Not if Lacey here is prepared to put up with me for longer. He has told me he has no intention of moving from Worthington Place for some weeks, and you already know how things stand between me and my sister. I may make a flying visit, just to pay my respects to my parents, you understand, but I shall return as soon as I may."

"I am delighted then, for I must tell you that I greatly value your company."

It was said with no side, for each regarded the other as a much admired friend, no more, Freddie having quickly realised that any amorous thoughts he'd had as a result of his uncle's remarks were now faded away. However, both the viscount and Dysart overheard her comment. Gideon was glad, because he knew Freddie would at times keep a watchful eye on his cousin when he was unable to do so. Dysart, not so familiar with the situation, was piqued, thinking Mr Hildebrand a far more worthy and therefore dangerous opponent than Major Saxby. What chance now would he have to woo his quarry with so affable a man present every hour of the day?

He wondered how long the two men planned to remain at Buxton Manor and indeed how long he might himself extend his visit. He had contrived to get rid of Thomas Mulberry for the most part, happy to relinquish riding with Patience when he had the rest of the days to engineer spending time with her. But now? And with Lacey there too? A man he loathed, for he was in possession of facts Dysart would not wish to have shared with the world at large. That Gideon had never yet done so, that he had for years kept his secret safe, bore little weight with a man who, had the positions been reversed, would not have hesitated to sacrifice the other for his own ends.

They hadn't seen much of each other of late, the viscount spending little time in London and Jasper Dysart only recently returning to Bath on a more permanent basis. That the former was aware of his iniquity he knew, for at the time they had been close friends and he had admitted as much. Gideon had been disgusted by his treatment of the girl in question — what was her name now? He couldn't recall. He was, however, completely ignorant of what had happened after he'd fled the capital, consideration for mother and child carrying no weight with him. What he did know, what he could see every time he looked into his erstwhile friend's eyes, was utter contempt. *I care little for that*, he told himself, but what he did care about was the relationship between Gideon and Patience. He suspected he would be hard put to get time alone with her while both men remained at Buxton Manor.

The next morning Gideon joined Patience and Thomas on their ride and the two men got along famously, joining together to tease her on her handling of the reins, unjust but irresistible. Andrew had taken Freddie and Jasper to fish for trout and the separate parties passed a pleasurable few hours. Coming together again, it was once more evident that the atmosphere was not entirely one of bonhomie. Clara did what she could, but in the end it was her husband who came to the rescue.

"I go to Bath in the morning, Dysart. Perhaps you would like to bear me company."

Though lacking in subtlety, it was said in a pleasant enough tone and the visitor had little choice but to accede, no excuse to remain being ready to hand. He was his ever urbane self and smiled politely. "An excellent suggestion, Buxton. It is time I returned. If you are planning to ride, then it would give me great pleasure to join you." That he had been outmanoeuvred Dysart was aware, but he would not concede defeat. Sooner or later Miss Worthington would return to Bath, and he would then resume his pursuit of her. Now more than ever he was determined to make her his.

With their unwelcome guest departed, the rest appreciated a week of unalloyed pleasure. Even Clara who, though there could be no doubt she was missing Andrew, succeeded in enjoying the house party. Her trill of laughter was heard everywhere, and never more so than when engaging with her children. Hide and seek was a favourite, even William seemingly unimpaired by his arm, which was strapped securely to his chest to prevent further damage. Edward was the most successful, on one occasion hiding in the old icehouse and having eventually to reveal his whereabouts after suffering with chattering teeth and trembling limbs for some considerable time, so long did he remain undiscovered.

Thomas Mulberry was several times invited to remain after the daily ride to join the rest, and Gideon could not see that Patience treated him any differently to anyone else or, indeed, himself. If there was romance in the air he was unable to detect it, but he could not curb a pang of envy when watching how close the two had become. It seemed no different than her friendship with Freddie, but Gideon had to admit to himself that he had fallen deeply in love.

I have none but myself to blame that she regards me with no more than a familial fondness, he told himself. Following an inauspicious beginning, though he blamed circumstance rather than any blunder on his part, he had tried in such a clumsy way to warn her against Dysart. She had resented his interference, no doubt about it, and, though they had since established an accord, it stood between them still. And who could blame her? To have offered a caution and then refused to explain why was, for one whose social graces were as a rule unimpeachable, ill-advised to say the very least. Had their positions been reversed, there was no doubt he would have demanded to know the circumstances.

What a fool he'd been. But Gideon was an honourable man. If Jasper was to be brought down, it would not be by his hand.

His determination was to protect Diana and Bella, safe for the time being in Combe. Who was to know whether or not Dysart would betray them once more if his own perfidy were to be exposed? No, in spite of his love for Patience, she would not hear it from his lips. There being no other way to exonerate himself, he must be content to remain her friend.

None of this did he allow to impact upon the general enjoyment, and it was with regret that after a week of simple amusements he declared he must return to Worthington Place, having pledged himself to his mother. It was a signal for the party to disperse, Freddie saying his visit home was now embarrassingly overdue and Patience not wishing to outstay her welcome. In the end, Clara declared she too would return to Bath. William was sufficiently recovered for her to have no qualms about leaving him and Edward with Nurse Dursley, and she was unfashionably pining for her husband.

Thomas was able to inform Patience that his sister Emily had formed no lasting attachment to Dysart and hoped in fact that the experience might have done her some good, perhaps even teaching her to be a little more wary in future.

"She felt no tendre for him?"

"She was flattered by his attention, of course, and any principled man would not have pursued her in such a manner, but my mother was able in her practical way to explain that he was in all probability amusing himself and if he said anything untoward she should report it to her immediately. Apparently he was once or twice a little incautious and it frightened Emily. Instead of being captivated by his charm, as no doubt he thought would be the case, she went straight to our parent. Mama told Papa, who gave him the hint and we saw no more of him thereafter. We must be grateful she has the protection of her family." The Mulberrys were looking forward now to the forthcoming wedding of Thomas's eldest sister. "I beg you will allow me to call upon you, should I find myself in Bath thereafter."

"It is something I shall anticipate with pleasure. Meanwhile, do please give my best wishes to your parents and thank them for their hospitality these past few weeks."

Thomas laughed. "I shall, of course, though you have done so yourself many times." He became serious for a moment. "If that man should pester you, I trust you know you have only to write and I will come immediately. He has the potential to be dangerous to any young girl."

"Young girl?" she laughed.

"You are not yet in your dotage, I believe."

Patience was grateful and said so. In addition, it gave her a warm feeling to know that she had several protectors who were ready and willing to guard her from harm. And when Mary moved permanently to Worthington Place and she needed to employ a companion, she would not have cause to feel alone in the world.

Upon her return to Bath, Patience received two letters, one which was waiting for her, the other arriving the following day. The first gave her cause for relief.

My dearest Miss Worthington,

It cannot have escaped your notice how attached to you I have become. I have told you so myself on many an occasion. I fear, though, that the time has come for me to relinquish my feelings, for you have made it clear they are not reciprocated. I will be returning to Oakenchurch towards the end of next week. My understanding is that you are at present out of town, so I will take my leave of you not in person, as I had hoped, but by means of this letter. Please be certain that if there is any way in which I can be of service to you in the future, you have only to let me know.

Yours

John Saxby

Patience looked at the date which had been penned at the top of the sheet and realised she had time still to write a reply before the major left town.

My dear Major Saxby,

It was kind of you indeed to inform me of your movements. I have but today returned to Bath and trust this will reach you before you yourself leave. While I cannot return those sentiments you have been so gracious as to bestow upon me, you must know that I value, have always valued, your friendship. I hope that we may meet again on some occasion, but there is one thing I would ask of you, if you would be so kind. It has been many weeks now since I left the vicarage, and in doing so I also left behind people with whom I had been acquainted my whole life. You know who they are. Should you meet some of them, as I am sure you will, I should be obliged if you would convey my best wishes and assure them they will always hold a place in my heart, as will you.

Patience Worthington

The second letter was one with which it was harder for Patience to deal. It came from Mary.

My dearest Patience,

Gideon — yes, I know, but he insists — returned to Worthington Place yesterday, as you are well aware. I am delighted that little William is doing so well and that Clara has felt able to move back to Upper Camden Place. Your cousin has kindly offered to drive me back to Bath *the day after tomorrow, and I trust you will be able to go on without me until then. He has insisted on sending this by courier so that you need not be anxious about being left alone for too long with only your maid to give you countenance.*

How very kind and typical of him, Patience thought, pausing for a moment before taking up the letter once more.

I shall be leaving all my paraphernalia here in what I have come to call my studio, there being far too much to keep removing from one place to another. Hester invites me to come as often as I like, as you well know, so I am hopeful that my next visit will not be long in coming when perhaps you may be wishful of visiting her yourself. While I am in Bath I will be more than content to occupy myself happily with my sketchbook, so you needn't think I will be looking about me for something to do.

It seems an age since last we met, my dearest. You will have much to tell me, I am sure.

Your loving friend,
Mary

Patience made no attempt to reply to this second letter. There was no need. What was needed was a solution to her dilemma, for nothing was more certain than that the time had come for her to let go the traces of her friend and companion so that she might lead her own life without obligation. There was no immediate answer to the problem, though her mind was greatly exercised wrestling with it.

The resolution, when it came, was from an entirely unexpected quarter. Visiting the Pump Room the next morning to catch up with her acquaintance, she chanced to meet Mrs Sacombe, who was keeping a watchful eye on her granddaughter, she being in close conversation with Simon Easton a few steps away. Fanny wasn't looking happy.

"My dear Miss Worthington. I am so glad to see you here today, for it gives me the opportunity of taking my leave of you in person."

"You are going away?"

"Sadly I must, for a few weeks at least. My daughter, my other daughter, Fanny's aunt you understand, has been laid low. She is a widow and her children no longer live at home, both having been married in the last year. She begs that I go and stay with her for a while and you will understand it is a request I cannot refuse, nor would I wish to do so."

"I am so sorry. I sincerely hope it is nothing of a lasting nature."

"Goodness me, no, but her doctor has advised that she takes things quietly. She has a lively mind, and without someone to bear her company I fear she would go quietly mad. Or even not quietly," she added with a wry smile.

"Then I am glad to have come home in time to see you, for I shall miss our times together. And Fanny? What of her?"

"That is the saddest part. I fear I must return her to her mother." Mrs Sacombe glanced quickly in the direction of the young couple. "Things were progressing so nicely. I feel sure they will make a match of it, if only given sufficient opportunity. Mr Easton has made no declaration as yet. I don't know, of course, but I believe he thinks it too soon, what with her being so young and not having been about very much at all. I honour him for that but would be very happy to see things settled between them. However…" She left the rest of the sentence unfinished and continued, "She is taking her leave of him now. That is why I have permitted them to stand a little apart. I am sure you can see neither is happy with the situation."

Patience had all the while been thinking, and before she could change her mind she said, "I wonder, Mrs Sacombe, how you would feel about entrusting Fanny to my care. I believe, no, I know Mary will be leaving me soon, and I find myself in a spot. This could be the answer both to your problem and mine."

"You wish my granddaughter to reside with you?" There was no denying the astonishment in the question.

Patience hastily backtracked. "I'm sorry. I have perhaps been too presumptuous. Forgive me."

But Mrs Sacombe was beaming. "It could be the very thing. You are far too young to act as chaperon, of course, but surely, with your maids to accompany you when you venture out, there can be no objection. My dear girl, it is a wonderful scheme. Come, child," she said, raising her voice to attract Fanny's attention.

"Yes, Grandmama?" she said, glancing plaintively at Simon before tearing herself away.

"There is no need for you to look so out of spirits. Miss Worthington here has come up with a solution to our problem." She went on to explain the situation, and a broad smile chased away the gloom from Fanny's pretty features. "Go on, child, you may tell your young man that you will not be leaving Bath in the foreseeable future. I shall write to Mama when we get home, but I do not anticipate any objection. She will be guided by me, I am sure."

Patience knew that Fanny would not remain with her forever. Perhaps just a few weeks. But for the time being the problem was resolved, and tomorrow she would be able to tell Mary what she knew she wanted to hear.

CHAPTER SIXTEEN

"What an age it seems since we saw each other, Mary. I had a delightful time at Buxton Manor. Those two boys would be sufficient to entertain anyone who is not above being pleased. I am aware there are many who consider a child's place is in the schoolroom, or at the very least kept away from visitors, but for my part they made my stay even more enjoyable. And Clara and Andrew have so many friends that I might have imagined myself still to be in town, for we were not without company for many moments, I can tell you. I don't think we spent a single evening alone after the second day. But what of you? Is my aunt well? I'm sorry to have missed my cousin, but I was with Mrs Sacombe when you arrived home. But more of that later." Patience paused for breath, her broad grin reflecting that of her friend. "Yes, I know. I do go on a bit. So, tell me."

"Hester is well, and I am delighted that my stay encouraged her once more to visit the gatehouse. She came each day, for she liked to sit and watch me at work, she said. Certainly the exertion seemed to do her no harm, so I was glad to be of service in that way."

"Yes, I suspect much of her inactivity in the past has been productive of boredom. Such a sad thing in one so intelligent who enjoys the company of others. You must have appeared like a ray of sunshine to her."

Mary blushed and demurred, but there was much in what Patience had said, and it was all the opening she needed to broach the subject of a change in their circumstances.

"It has become increasingly obvious to me that your talent has become not merely a hobby but an obsession. It is time, I think, since you have been invited to do so, for you to return to Worthington Place to live there permanently. You are receiving due payment for your work, which will enable you to occupy the cottage and pay for your keep with no obligation to Hester and Gideon. Indeed, I think the obligation, if one exists, may well be on her side."

The colour rushed to Mary's face, and she raised her hand in objection and spoke with a trace of anger in her voice. "There is no way I will leave you, Patience. You should know that, for we made a pact when we left Oakenchurch that we would remain together."

"Indeed we did, and it was what circumstances demanded at the time."

"And how pray have those circumstances altered?"

"Yours because there is now someone whose need of you is greater than mine. You have said yourself what a difference your presence has made to Hester. My own position has not changed so much, but something has arisen whereby there is a temporary solution to my predicament, and I consider it timely to say the least."

Mary was at pains to know in what way things could have changed to such an extent without her knowledge, and Patience explained how it had come about that Fanny Sacombe was to live with her for a while in Lansdown Crescent.

"It was arranged only yesterday and I was with them discussing the details earlier today, which is why I wasn't at home when you arrived. Mrs Sacombe is called away to her other daughter for an extended visit and Fanny will be here tomorrow." She smiled again. "I believe the old lady was loath to drag her grandchild away from Bath at this time. You will not be surprised to learn that Mr Easton has become very particular in his attentions and it is a match that would be welcome, young as they both are. However, he has not yet declared himself, so you may see what a position it leaves them in."

Mary could indeed see and was sympathetic, but replied, "That's all very well, but the time will come when she will return to her grandmother."

"It will, of course, but by then I hope to have engaged a suitable companion. No, don't object, Mary. It was inevitable that something would arise to part us, though I didn't expect it to be so soon. How would it have been if I had become betrothed to Major Saxby, for instance? I know it was what you wished for me at one time, and I am certain you would not have consented to become a member of my household in such a situation."

It was the plain truth, and Mary had no way to counter the argument. She had always believed she would be the one left, not the leaver, but she could see that Patience would brook no challenge, nor in her heart of hearts did she wish to offer one.

"So you see how fortuitous it is that you have left all your materials and will have only your wardrobe to convey. Shall we go on a shopping spree before you leave? I'm sure Fanny will wish to go with us. In the meantime, though, I suggest you write immediately to my aunt, for I am certain no-one will be more delighted than she to know of your coming."

Mary went off in a happy haze to pen her letter, and Patience was satisfied that things had gone as well as she could have expected.

Fanny arrived in Lansdown Crescent early the next day, her grandmother anxious to make an early start on her journey to her daughter. Her delight in her new bedchamber was evident, Patience having put a comb, a silver-handled brush, a mirror of the same design and a few other items on the dresser, together with some fresh flowers in the same yellow that decorated the room.

"This is so pretty, Patience. I don't know how to thank you."

"Sadly it doesn't have the nicest view, being at the front of the house, but I agree, the interior more than makes up for that. I have not given you Mary's room, for there is no saying that she may not, from time to time, wish to spend a few days in Bath and I would like her to be in familiar surroundings. In any case, she doesn't leave us until tomorrow."

"No, of course not. I wouldn't dream. And this suits me admirably, I promise you."

"In that case, while your maid is unpacking your things, perhaps we might join Mary, who I know is anxious to purchase one or two things before she leaves."

No further encouragement was needed and the shopping spree was everything they could have wished, Miss Petersham being unable to resist adding one or two brushes, some paints and some canvases to her purchases. A gift for Hester was found in a shop they had never before visited, a beautifully decorated fan. Mary knew it would be useful for someone who felt the heat as much as the viscountess did. One or two personal items were added also. Fanny discovered some light blue satin ribbon of exactly the shade to match her favourite muslin day dress. "I also have a straw bonnet which is begging to be refurbished. It will be just the thing."

Patience found what she wanted in the form of some notepaper. Major Saxby's letter, or rather her reply, had made her realise that she had been remiss in not keeping in touch with some of her closer acquaintance in Oakenchurch, and she had little doubt as well that she and Mary would form a regular correspondence. Though the distance between Worthington

Place and Lansdown Crescent was not great, it was unlikely that the journey would be made frequently. She would have been less than human had she not wished to be kept abreast of what was going on. In addition, she had the intention of embarking on an exchange of letters between herself and Thomas Mulberry, for they had much in common and it was a friendship she did not wish to allow to dwindle.

When Gideon arrived the next morning, he received such a welcome as to warm his heart. He wished it had been his cousin he was taking back to Worthington Place, for he desired to see more of her than present circumstances allowed. However, with Mary to bear his mother company, he would have more time available to visit the town without it impinging on his conscience. He held out little hope for the fulfilment of his dream but he would, if he could, contrive to spend more time with Patience, for he was never happier than in her company. She hugged Mary, shook Gideon's hand and waved them off from the front step, Fanny at her side. Ten minutes later Simon Easton came to pay a call, much to that young lady's delight, followed but a few minutes later by Jasper Dysart. Though he received a polite enough welcome, his hostess wished him elsewhere.

"Miss Worthington, Miss Sacombe, Mr Easton, I bid you good day. Such a fine one as it is, I wondered if you might enjoy a walk in Sydney Gardens."

Fanny, so pleased to receive such an early visit from Simon, was quick to acquiesce. Too quick for Patience, who would have declined the invitation. The four set off immediately, falling naturally into pairs and, while Dysart tried to slow their pace so as to distance themselves from the others, she was having none of it. She didn't wish to be alone with him, and more importantly, it was her obligation to keep a watchful eye on her charge.

Her companion smiled, but it wasn't the sort of smile she appreciated, particularly when he said suggestively, "You must be able to see that they have eyes only for each other."

"All the more reason to stay close. You must know that in her grandmother's absence I am acting as chaperon to Miss Sacombe, and it is my responsibility to see that she is not put in a vulnerable situation."

Dysart missed his step and she looked at him enquiringly. She couldn't know how he wondered if she had been the recipient of Lacey's confidence. He recovered quickly, realising had that been the case she would in all probability have refused him entry to the house, and certainly would not have gone walking with him, but for a moment he had been shaken out of his complacency. "You are too young and beautiful to act as anyone's chaperon," he countered.

"Nonsense!" was all the reply he received, she now being extremely irritated. He used all his charm in an attempt to recover ground, unable to accept that the fair lady would have none of him. What's more, he liked her spirit.

She, on the other hand, was wondering how she could contrive to give him a hint strong enough that he would withdraw his pursuit of her. Obviously he did not respond to the usual niceties and seemed immune to her disapproval of him. As independent as she was, she couldn't help admitting (but only to herself) that she would have welcomed the protection of Gideon Worthington or Thomas Mulberry, or indeed Freddie Hildebrand. She could only hope that Freddie would return soon to Bath and could perhaps advise her in her dilemma.

In her efforts to keep her young visitor well-entertained — and to give her as much opportunity as possible to see Mr Easton — Patience went more frequently to the Pump Room and the Lower Assembly Rooms on Terrace Walk. In this respect she was successful, for though she took her duties to heart they were places where the young couple were able to communicate in such a way as to be beyond reproach. It would not be long, she was certain, before that young man declared himself, and she was unsurprised when one day he took her aside to ask her advice.

"Miss Worthington, you cannot be unaware of my feeling for Miss Sacombe. Her beauty, her manners, her smile. All are enough to turn any man's head. I cannot be sure, though, that she thinks of me in the same way. She treats everyone with equal courtesy, and I would be mortified to embarrass her by making a declaration she did not want to receive."

Men can be so blind, Patience thought. *Particularly young men.* But his youth would not be detrimental in this relationship, for he suited Fanny exactly.

She was given no opportunity to reply, for he carried on without pause. "You have always been so kind to me. I would wish to take counsel with my parents, but my family home is far north of here, and I cannot tear myself away from Fanny's side. Tell me, if you will, do you think my suit will be welcomed?"

"I truly believe she will be more than happy to receive an offer from you, sir."

"Then perhaps I may call on you tomorrow, if you permit."

Patience teased him for a moment or two, declaring that as she stood in loco parentis she would be unable to leave them alone for him to make any proposal, but she took immediate pity on him when he looked so crestfallen that it was hard to hide a smile. "No, don't look so downhearted, Mr Easton. Society dictates that a man must at least be given an opportunity to announce his intentions. Do come tomorrow, by all means, and I shall contrive to have an excuse to leave the room for five minutes. Will that be sufficient, do you think?"

His smiling face and the gratitude with which he expressed himself assured her that it would.

Patience had been less successful in shaking the attentions of Jasper Dysart, her frequent visits to public places with Fanny giving him ample opportunity to engage with her. He did not under the circumstances even have to contrive excuses to visit her at home. While she refused resolutely to ride with him or go out in his carriage, often using her charge as an excuse, she could find no way to rebuff him entirely. He seemed immune to her hints.

Unknown to Patience, Dysart had been standing behind her and had overheard some of her conversation with Simon Easton. Knowing therefore that she would be at home the next day, he too paid a visit to Lansdown Crescent. His timing was perfect, for he had stood in the shadows waiting for the younger man's arrival and waited patiently for him to depart. As Simon bounded down the steps and walked away in a happy haze, Dysart strolled across the road and rapped on the knocker. He was shown into the drawing room, where Patience and Fanny were in a state of excited animation, already discussing how they would convey the news to her family.

"I must go immediately and write to my mother," Fanny had said at the exact moment Dysart entered. "Oh! Good morning, sir. Please excuse me, for I have to go to my room." She swept past him, leaving poor Patience to deal with this thorn in her side.

"I had not expected a visit from you today, sir. Do sit down and I shall ring for some refreshment."

"No, I want nothing, thank you, though that is not strictly true. Miss Worthington. Patience." He moved closer. Far too close for her liking. "I come to you, a man passionately in love. It seems, if I am to read the signs correctly, that your charge will soon be leaving you as Miss Petersham has already done." He grasped her hands. She tried to draw them away, but his grip was firm. "Allow me, I beg of you, to take your life into my care. I ask nothing more than for you to be my wife."

Her recalcitrant sense of humour caused her to think that this was far more than enough, but it would seem he was not to be deterred. As she stepped back, he followed her. "Release me, if you please. I cannot talk to you standing like this."

Her matter-of-fact manner shook him out of his complacency, and he did as she asked.

"I am not unmindful of the honour you do me, sir, but please accept that I do not look for marriage. I am content with my lot and must ask you not importune me further."

Dysart could never be long in her company without his passion rising to the fore, and today was no exception. Fire burned in his eyes, and instead of taking rejection and leaving quietly as any gentleman would, he gripped her shoulders and dragged her into his arms. She struggled vainly but all at once subsided. He thought he had won but he could not see, as she could, that the door had opened. The footman entered and announced with a slight cough, "Mr Hildebrand, miss."

Freddie stepped in and Dysart stepped back, the flame in his eyes now one of anger.

"Freddie, how good to see you," Patience said, more relieved than she cared to admit and cross that she had allowed herself to be drawn into such a situation. "Mr Dysart was just leaving. Good day, sir, and thank you for your call."

He had no option but to go. She wished she could feel reassured that it was the last she would see of him.

"Freddie, you have no idea how pleased I am that you have come just now."

"Haven't I just, Patience. I could see what was happening before your man announced me. Whatever possessed you to allow yourself to be alone with that blackguard? No, don't cry," he said as the tears began to fall upon her cheeks. "Here, sit down and tell me all about it. If you wish, that is. Not meaning to pry, but it seems to me you may be in need of some help."

She poured the whole story into his ears, starting with news of Fanny and Simon's betrothal and explaining how she had been caught off her guard when Miss Sacombe had gone to her room. "And you must not reprimand her for leaving me alone with him. She was far too excited to realise and was thinking only of writing her letter."

"She ought to have known better," he said, a little harshly.

Her sense of humour reasserting itself, Patience said, "No, of course not. In her eyes I am a spinster of a certain age who must be beyond the very idea of romance."

"Balderdash. Seems to me every time I see you you're warding off the attentions of some suitor or other."

"It's kind of you to say so, Freddie, and perhaps I'm not at my last prayers yet, but I will not have Fanny mortified by these events, so you must promise not even to mention them to her."

He gave in grudgingly but said, "Well, it's a jolly good thing I'm back in Bath. I've not yet been to Worthington Place, but my plan was to stay there as before. However, if you'd prefer me to remain in town for a few days, that can easily be arranged."

"That is kind of you indeed but not necessary. I shall be more on my guard in the future. But tell me if you will, Freddie, why did you call him a blackguard?" she asked innocently, hoping to gain some information from him.

"I'd have thought that was obvious. Gentlemen don't make a habit of forcing their attentions on young women, no matter how enamoured they might be."

"Is that all?"

"All! Ain't that enough?"

"I thought you might have learned more from my cousin as to what it is that caused the animosity between them."

"No, and I'm not asking. When Gideon wants to confide in me, he will."

With that she had to be content, though it still rankled that she had been given a warning without an explanation.

"Tell you what, why don't you come with me to Worthington Place? Spend a few days there. Get you out of Dysart's way."

"You are forgetting Miss Sacombe."

"Well, bring her along too."

"What a lovely man you are. I couldn't, though. You must see how cruel it would be to tear her away from Simon at this time."

"Then I shall remain in Bath."

She managed to talk him out of it, though it took all her powers of persuasion. Secretly, he had the intention to visit far more often than he might otherwise have done.

Fanny came back into the room, her letter written, and Patience said with some contrition, "You will forgive me, dearest, but I have made known your intentions to Mr Hildebrand."

She blushed prettily and accepted his congratulations on her forthcoming nuptials. "It will be a while yet. I am not even yet properly out in Society, and I must of course have Papa's consent. My home is thankfully clear now of chicken pox, but Grandmama remains with my aunt. Mr Easton plans to call on my father, and he wishes also to travel to his own home to inform his parents before any official announcement is made."

"Then it will be our secret, Miss Sacombe."

Freddie took his leave of them but assured Patience he would return to Bath in a day or so, and that in the meantime she should take care of herself.

"Whatever did he mean by that?" asked Fanny.

"Nothing, dearest. Now tell me again, what exactly did Simon say to you?"

Fanny needed no further encouragement.

CHAPTER SEVENTEEN

Later that day, alone in her room, Patience wrote to Thomas Mulberry.

My dear friend,

I have been back in Bath for some time now and must tell you I am missing our daily conversations. And our rides. By the time this reaches you, I calculate there will be but a few days until your sister's wedding. Please convey my best wishes to your family as before.

She paused, not sure how to continue, but decided truth was the best thing.

I pray you will forgive the presumption, but I write because I need a friend in whom to confide. You will know how unwelcome are the attentions to me of Jasper Dysart, but he has been persistent in pursuing me since my return to town. Earlier today I had the misfortune, due to my own stupidity, to find myself alone with him. You may imagine how he behaved, for you have seen for yourself what a man he is in his dealings with your younger sister. He grasped hold of me and I was unable to push him away. Thankfully, Freddie Hildebrand chose that very moment to arrive and rescued me from a difficult situation. I was more angry than afraid, and you need not fear that I shall allow myself to be placed again in such a compromising position. I tell you only because it eases my mind to speak of it, rather than hold it inside like a poisonous pill. Freddie has expressed the intention of coming often to Bath (he stays at Worthington Place) and I know my cousin too will visit. Then, of course, Clara and Andrew are in Upper Camden Place, so you must not think I am without protection.

I am sorely tempted to tear up this letter, now I have been able to express myself and thus relieve my somewhat pent-up feelings. I shall not do so because I am hoping we will become regular correspondents, and I would not wish to have secrets from you.

Do write to me after the wedding and tell me all about it and, if you should happen at any time to see Edward and William, let them know that I am practising hard at jackstraws for when next we meet.

With affection,

Patience

Feeling better for having put her sentiments into words, Patience, composed once more, went to join Fanny for supper. She was able to set her own problems aside as the young girl could talk of nothing, or rather no-one, other than her betrothed.

The following day, Simon took his leave of them to journey north. The day after that Mrs Sacombe, in response to her granddaughter's letter, arrived back in Bath.

"Good gracious, Grandmama, I had no expectation of seeing you so soon," Fanny said when summoned to her side.

"Then you ought not to have sent me such an exciting message," the old lady replied, her affection so obvious in her smile.

"And what of your daughter, Mrs Sacombe? Is she much improved?"

"You haven't met my Sukie, have you? She's not a bit like Fanny's mama. I found when I arrived that it was nothing near as serious as she had described, only that she was suffering mostly from ennui and wanted some company. I was that cross with her, I can tell you, dragging me away at a time like this.

Not that she knew it was a time like this, to be sure, but she's a bit too good at considering only herself, I'm afraid."

Patience was amused at Mrs Sacombe's obvious indignation, but it meant of course that a problem which she had thought resolved once more rose to the fore. "You will be wanting Fanny to come back to you, of course?"

The old lady looked contrite, because she was only too aware of the position in which she was putting her young friend. "When you are ready, naturally. There is no immediate hurry, but I would like to take my granddaughter to her mother now that the pox has passed and she is able to return home. I do have someone I could put forward to you. A girl who until recently was chaperon to a young woman who has herself recently married and no longer requires her. But I don't like to advance someone whom you have not met, and perhaps you have a lady among your own acquaintance?"

"I do not, and would rather by far act upon recommendation than have to advertise in the newspaper. Do please give me her direction and I shall write to her. Does she reside in Bath?"

Mrs Sacombe sent Fanny to fetch her address book and was able to speak more freely in her absence. "In Chippenham, so I dare say it will take little time for her to come if you should choose to interview her. I am so sorry to serve you this way when you have been so very kind to my girl."

"Nonsense. I hope I am amiable enough to rub along with most people, and in any case the arrangement with Fanny was only temporary. Don't give it another thought."

"Very well, but you must know how grateful I am to you, for who knows what might have been the outcome had I been forced to take Fanny away?"

"I feel certain it would have been the same, though perhaps it might have taken a little longer. They will be happy together,

I'm sure. I shall leave Fanny with you now and send her maid to accompany her back to Lansdown Crescent in an hour or two, if that suits. You must have much to talk about."

The smile returned and Patience left immediately, anxious to write to Miss Muker as quickly as possible. She received a reply in the form of Miss Abigail Muker herself, who was keen to save time by presenting herself in person rather than on the page. She was a no-nonsense young woman of perhaps three-and-thirty years, well-experienced in her profession and, to the delight of her new employer, blessed with a dry sense of humour. Patience engaged her on the spot. Abigail had no cause to return to Chippenham, where she had been staying with a friend. Her luggage was sent for and Fanny returned to the bosom of her grandmama.

Things had worked out admirably, but the whole series of events gave Patience pause once more to consider her own future. Sitting one morning with Clara, she told her cousin of her intention to return to Oakenchurch.

"You're leaving Bath!" she exclaimed, incredulous.

Patience laughed. "Only for a short while, but there are people I would wish to see again. When my father was alive — " she paused as her emotions threatened to overcome her — "I used to visit his parishioners with him, and sometimes without. I would do so again, not to encroach on the domain of the new incumbent, but to renew friendships. And, when I do return to Bath, it is my intention to do some work with the poor of this parish."

"But you are a woman!"

Both laughed at the explosive comment, Clara's trill as infectious as ever.

"And you are an old-fashioned one. Why should I not be useful, if I can? I thought you of all people would understand my need to be doing."

Clara, though she contrived to conceal it, was overcome with sadness. She had so hoped to find a suitable match for her cousin, wishing her the same happiness she had herself. It seemed not to be what she wanted.

How wrong she was. Patience had once had only her mother and father. They were gone now, but she had discovered an aunt for whom she had the utmost respect and affection, a cousin with two boys whom frankly she adored and another cousin who, well, the less she thought about Gideon the better. But he was a good friend. They were all good friends. They were the extended family she hadn't known she possessed, and they had only served to make her realise how much she wanted a family of her own. None of this did she confide to Clara, who was forced to accept that Patience would make her own way. She could not but admire her for her strength of character.

Having written to Reverend Moorcroft, good manners dictating that Patience inform him of her impending visit to Oakenchurch, she had received a reply begging her to treat her old home as before: *You must know the vicarage is a spacious property, and we have no children of our own to fill it.* Having no other arrangements in place and needing somewhere to reside, she accepted gratefully. And so it was that she once more left Lansdown Crescent for a stay in the country.

Abigail was fully cognisant of the situation and her matter-of-fact attitude had helped pass the journey, but Patience found her courage almost failing her when the coach in which she and her companion were travelling pulled to a halt in front of the house. Not only had some considerable time passed since last she was there, but much also had occurred. All that faded away as she returned to her childhood home. There was no time for reminiscing, though, as the reverend and his wife appeared at the front door to greet them before even a foot had reached the ground. She was charmed by them both, he putting her much in mind of her father, though several years his junior. Mrs Moorcroft was nothing like her mother, but a homely woman who could be seen immediately to be one of life's all-embracing characters.

"Doubtless you will be hungry after your journey. Do go directly to your rooms if you wish to freshen up, and then join us at the table. Joseph will have it that I always serve up too much, but you can't change the habits of a lifetime, can you?"

Patience, who had anticipated feeling uncomfortable, found that she straight away settled into the altered situation, though she did shed a few tears as she fingered the curtains at the window of her bedchamber, chosen with such care so many years ago when Mama was still alive. She looked out through the glass, from where she could see the small graveyard. Tomorrow she would visit her parents' graves, but for today she would return the kindness of her hosts and behave as her father would have expected her to. With dignity.

"You could not have chosen a better time to come," said Reverend Moorcroft. "If my understanding is correct and you wish to be of assistance, I can tell you that we have had an epidemic running through the parish which has laid low many of our members. Sadly we lost two, but the rest are on the mend or entirely recovered. However, as happens at such times, the call for comfort is increased and I have been struggling to call upon everyone as frequently as I would like."

"I hardly see him except when he comes in for his dinner, and then he's so hungry he barely has time to talk to me — and him complaining I give him too much! You just watch and see how much he leaves," Martha said, laughing, and it was true. Joseph made a hearty meal. When it was over and they sat companionably in the parlour, he turned once more to Patience.

"Perhaps you will consult with me in the morning and we can divide the community between us. I can walk to those who live nearby, freeing up the gig for you to visit the rest who live further afield. Or the other way around, if you prefer."

"There will be many who will come into both categories, so I leave it to you to decide the best method. One way or another I mean to visit everyone I knew before I leave, which probably signifies everyone on your list. Abigail is resolved to come with me. My only concern is that I don't encroach, so you must tell me if I presume too much, sir. I would not repay your kindness by giving offence."

"Foolish girl. You must know from your father's work here before that all aid is most gratefully appreciated."

The day dawned with hazy sunshine and Patience, donning a shawl, went before breakfast to kneel at the graves of her parents. She looked upon her mother's headstone as she had on so many occasions in the past, only this time it was different. She smiled.

"It would seem, Mama, that there was much about you I did not know. You are aware you have a niece, Clara, for you wrote to me of her. She is like you in many ways, and never more so than when she laughs and I can imagine you standing beside me. She has a very fine husband and two delightful boys. Your sisters both passed many years ago."

Almost as if Lizzie Worthington could hear her, Patience hesitated before continuing.

"Papa's brother, too, is deceased, but I met his wife. I perfectly understand why you and she were such good friends, for you would have dealt well together. She confided much to me, far more than you ever did. Not a criticism, Mama. I perfectly understand that you had long left your old life behind you. You might, though, like to know that Hester regrets that circumstances meant you could no longer continue as before and that her anger against you at the time has long dissipated. What a brave girl you were, flouting Society in such a way. Did you know that Lord Lacey has been dead these many years? Papa did not, for he too left me a letter, instructing me to seek him out. Instead I found his son, my cousin Gideon. You may be glad to know we have become good friends.

"I am at present living in Bath but have returned home to visit some old friends. I shall come and sit with you again before I leave. You and Papa have always been my inspiration and will, I am certain, continue to be so."

Patience moved to her father's grave but found, in death, as in life, that companionable silence was a solace to her. Rising after a while, she returned to the house to discuss the day's activities with Joseph Moorcroft.

At the end of a week, Patience decided her work here was done. The experience had been something of a two-edged sword, on the one hand confirming that helping people was in her blood and on the other that Joseph was adequately able, with Martha's aid, to serve his community. She was convinced now that her future lay in helping others, but where and how that would take place Patience couldn't be sure. Abigail had been of immense support, and would no doubt be a willing participant in whatever form of assistance her employer undertook.

It was time to leave. In between calls, Patience had had much time for reflection, often at Lizzie's graveside, and the seed of an idea began to grow. She had considered what her mother's position might have been all those years ago, had her father not come to her rescue. There might be any number of women who had fallen upon hard times. It was an avenue she intended to explore upon her return to Bath.

Her leave-taking from her previous neighbours was less emotionally fraught than the first time. Then she had thought never to return and, overwhelmed with grief, had given little consideration to its impact. This time she knew almost with certainty that she wouldn't come back. She saw John Saxby once during her visit, encountering him at the home of one of the parishioners. He had escorted her back to the vicarage but thankfully had made no reference to their previous situation, merely wishing her well and taking his leave. Her life here had been but one chapter, and the pages were turning. This time, as the carriage drove away from Oakenchurch, Patience did not look back.

The house in Lansdown Crescent felt strangely quiet, but welcoming nonetheless, and Patience came to the realisation that she now regarded this place as her home. It suited her well and would be a good base for the foreseeable future.

"Tomorrow I shall make it my business to visit the parish priest. There must surely be a home for fallen women in Bath. Or maybe there is some other way of tracing these poor girls, for not all will have been promiscuous. Some, I am certain, will have been the victim of circumstances. For today, though, Abigail, I am content to be home."

"How do you intend to be of help to them? You have told me yourself you do not have the funds to support them."

Patience laughed. "In all honesty, I have no idea, but that is no excuse for doing nothing. Truly I don't know, but I am determined to try. For instance, and I hope my father does not turn in his grave to hear me, I think the suggestion of finding solace in prayer will not serve at all. These women will need something far more practical. It may be that we can locate benefactors who will support our cause." She'd picked up some correspondence from a tray in the hall, mostly invitations, but one was in Thomas Mulberry's hand and she said, "Please excuse me for a while. I would like to read this straight away."

"Of course. In any case, I must fetch a shawl. The evenings are beginning to feel chilly, don't you think, now that the season is so advanced."

Abigail left the room and Patience unfolded the letter, reflecting how lucky she was to have found a woman with a practical bent and to whom she had no need to explain herself.

My dearest friend,

I am in Bath and you are flown! No matter. I shall, having been invited, adjourn to Worthington Place until I hear from you, Gideon having extended an open invitation when we were at Buxton Manor. I just pray that he too has not gone from home.

You will be pleased, I am sure, to learn that my sister's wedding went off without incident and to the delight of all involved. Even more reassuring is the fact that Emily has made the acquaintance of a young man much nearer to her in age than Dysart and by far a more suitable companion. I doubt anything will come of it, for these are her first tentative steps, but we are all happy to know that there are no lingering feelings of guilt or pain.

Patience put a hand to her cheek, thinking how, had the girl not been so protected, she might easily have become one of the number she would herself be seeking out the next day.

Do write to me upon your return. I shall remain with Worthington until then, unless circumstances dictate otherwise.
Yours with much affection,
Thomas Mulberry

She was sorry to have missed Thomas but glad to know he was close at hand and they would have the opportunity to meet again soon. With a sigh of contentment at having found a direction, she laid aside the letter to answer later. For now she would walk around the garden, her thoughts racing to tomorrow and the path she had chosen. She knew not where it might lead but, filled with purpose, her heart swelled. A new chapter had indeed begun.

CHAPTER EIGHTEEN

Thomas had been only two days at Worthington Place, and Freddie with him, when they returned from shooting to find Gideon pacing the library in some distress.

"What is it, man?"

"Bad news?" Freddie asked, for he could see a note in Gideon's hand.

"No. Yes. Possibly. Gentlemen, I'm afraid I must leave you to your own devices for a while."

"Oh, come on, Gideon, you've known me long enough to be sure you will not get away that easily without explanation. Is there something we can do to aid you? You seem uncommonly distressed."

Lacey looked from the face of one to the other, both men so obviously anxious to do what they could to help, and made a decision. Circumstances were such that they might indeed be able to be of assistance and, if that were the case, he would beg them to come with him, for the note he had received was from Diana Painswick. Bella had gone missing earlier in the day. Diana had thought she was playing with a friend in the village, for that had been her intention. It was something she did often, but when she had not returned within two hours Diana had gone to fetch her. She had never arrived and everyone was out searching for her, but it had been hours. There were no more details, only that she begged him to come if he could. The poor girl was obviously distraught.

"I must ride to Combe immediately. I'll explain as we go to the stables."

Gideon sent a footman running ahead to have Thunderbolt saddled up together with two other horses which would suit Freddie and Thomas. He explained that Miss Painswick was living under his protection in the nearby village and that her child could not be found. What his friends made of this he could only imagine. For the moment it wasn't important, though it was likely they came to the obvious but wrong conclusion. Dysart's name was not mentioned. No questions were asked and the three set off at a spanking pace, riding hard. It was by now past one o'clock, Diana having searched fruitlessly for a while before dashing off her letter to Gideon. They kept up with him, just, Thunderbolt delighted at being given his head. He skidded suddenly to a halt, and they almost flew past, so unexpected was it.

Gideon flung himself from his horse as the young woman came rushing out of the cottage. He grasped her hands and said reassuringly, "Don't worry, my dear. We shall find her. Tell me what you know."

Diana's shoulders relaxed a little, but she looked questioningly at his companions.

"My friends, Hildebrand and Mulberry. They insisted on coming to help if they could."

"She's been gone so long, Gideon," Diana said, turning a brave face to him, but her lip was quivering. Freddie had met her before, some years ago in London. He was astonished to find her here in this out-of-the-way place. Thomas, for his part, thought he had never seen a more beautiful young woman.

"She's probably fallen asleep somewhere. Perhaps she went off to pick some flowers and got lost." He turned to the other two. "The men of the village will be out on foot. Here," he said, bending down and drawing a map in the dust on the ground. "I will ride to the copse. You, Freddie, go along the road in this direction and perhaps you, Thomas, could go cross country into this field. Bella has played there before and she may have wandered too far and become tired."

"But she's only four, Gideon," Diana wailed. "How could she go so far?"

"You know what a little adventuress she is. Go inside now, in case she comes trotting in through the back, for I wouldn't put it past her. The rest of us will meet back here in an hour, as we shall have no way of knowing which of us has been successful."

He had said "has been" rather than "may have been" to reassure Bella's mother, but he was truly worried. He covered it as best he could by adopting an air of assurance, and the three set off in their different directions.

An hour later, Gideon and Freddie returned to see Thomas striding across the field, leading his horse and carrying the child in his arms. Diana, waiting at the door, saw him also and ran across the road. The gate through which Thomas had earlier ridden his horse was a few yards away and Gideon raced to open it, leading the gelding back while the other carried his precious burden.

"She is unconscious, Mrs Painswick, but alive. I fear she may have concussion, for I found her in a ditch into which it appeared she had fallen and knocked herself out."

"Take her inside, Tom," Gideon said. "I will fetch the doctor, and Freddie and I will ride about the village and tell the rest that she has been recovered and return here soon."

He did as bidden and laid the child gently on the sofa in the parlour. She was very pale, her colour in stark contrast to the patches of dirt on her face.

"I cannot thank you enough, sir. I truly believed she was lost to me."

"Her breathing is shallow but steady. I feel sure she will survive, Mrs Painswick."

"It is not Mrs but Miss, as I am sure you must have realised."

He made no comment. What could he say? But he had never been more surprised than to learn that Gideon had set up his mistress and love child in this village so close to home, he supposed for convenience. He was disappointed in the man, for it was plain Diana was of gentle birth, not that it should make any difference, but why on earth had he not made an honest woman of her?

Freddie arrived back at the cottage, having reassured two men in the village whom he'd found searching behind the hedgerow and charged them with the task of informing the rest that all was well. Gideon, close on his heels, said, "The doctor will be here in a matter of minutes, Diana. He was pausing only to collect his bag and, being quicker than him, I ran ahead to relieve your mind if I could. Ah, here he comes now."

Diana refused to leave her daughter's side. "She will be frightened if she awakes and I am not here."

The doctor, knowing her to be a sensible young woman, raised no objection. The three men walked along the lane to where they had tethered their horses to wait for the prognosis. It was Freddie who broke the silence that had fallen upon them, his tone of sarcasm making Gideon wince.

"Diana Painswick, eh? Nice girl. I remember you had a thing for her. Never thought to wonder what had happened to her. Well, now I can see. Very convenient bringing her to Combe, where you could come and go as you please."

"Don't be a fool, Freddie. You must know that Bella isn't my daughter."

"Well, I admit to being surprised, but what other significance could I put upon it?" he answered, his tone only a little less mocking than before.

Gideon, on the point of flaring up, realised that the conclusion his friend had come to was the obvious one so, instead of allowing his hurt to overwhelm him, he paused and stroked Thunderbolt's neck before taking a breath and saying, "Yes, I can see that's how it would appear, and I fear I must put you in possession of the facts, even though I promised Diana I never would betray her confidence."

"You mean you haven't betrayed her already?" Thomas asked quietly, up until now only an observer.

"I have not, nor will I ever do so. I am not the villain of this piece, Mulberry, but Freddie is right. Five years ago I fell in love with her, only there was another whose charms it seemed were greater than mine." He sounded bitter. "Diana told me how she felt about him. She was besotted and later, when he took the worst advantage and then abandoned her, she came to me, not knowing which way to turn."

"Her parents?" Freddie asked.

"Would have nothing to do with her. They said she had brought disgrace down upon their heads. My opinion is that they should have taken better care of her but no, they blamed her. Their reputation was ruined. What would their friends say? You may imagine how well that sat with me."

"So you brought her here," said Thomas. "I see. Are you still in love with her?"

"No, it was more the infatuation of a young man and died as quickly as it had arisen. But I am excessively fond of her, and of Bella too."

"And they will remain here for the foreseeable future?"

"Diana has no wish to be elsewhere. There were some curious glances initially, naturally, and some of the villagers looked sideways at me, having drawn the same conclusion as you two. But over time they have accepted her as one of their own, in spite of the difference in background. Even my regular visits here are not regarded as extraordinary, and I have never spent the night here. I believe that has contributed in putting people's doubts to rest. No, she is content to remain here, for Bella is thriving. In a year or two, when she is old enough, I shall engage someone to teach her those things a girl of gentle birth should know, and I hope eventually to bring her into the world where she belongs."

"And this villain, presumably he plays no further part in her life?" Thomas asked.

"No, none."

"It is unfortunate that he plays a part in ours," said Freddie.

Gideon looked at him keenly. "You have guessed, then."

"How could I not? You and he were the best of friends. I never knew what occurred to cause a rift between you, but I understand now your antipathy towards him. Jasper Dysart has much to answer for."

"Dysart!" The word exploded from Thomas's lips.

"I'm right, aren't I, Gideon?"

"You are, and you can imagine my feelings when I saw him return to Bath a few months ago. I have warned Diana, though I am certain he won't come looking for her."

"Does she love him still?" Freddie asked, incredulous.

"She neither loves nor hates him. I am happy to say she regards him with indifference. Not that we ever discuss him, but I know her whole being is focused upon her child. She has no time to waste on futile emotion."

Freddie looked at his friend earnestly. "I must beg your forgiveness. For a moment I thought the worst of you. I should have known better. Have I not been acquainted with you for long enough to be sure you would have done the right thing by Diana if the child had been yours? Instead, and in spite of the circumstances, you have secured her future. I salute you."

Gideon warmly wrung the hand that was offered him, relieved after all this time to have shared the burden of his secret. He looked up the road, his attention caught by something out of the corner of his eye.

"The doctor is leaving. Come, let us see how little Bella does. I rely on you both to protect me from Diana's wrath, for now that all is well, as I am certain it will be, she will surely berate me for having exposed her."

Gideon may have been joking, but he was nonetheless concerned at what Diana's reaction might be to him disclosing their secret, albeit to the most trustworthy of friends.

"Uncle Gideon, my head hurts," said the little girl as they entered the cottage. Neither Freddie nor Thomas was surprised to see such a softening as he approached her and laid his hand gently upon her forehead.

"I'm sure it does, my sweet, but buck up if you can, for I have brought two handsome gentlemen to meet you."

Bella stirred and looked past him to see the two standing with broad smiles upon their faces. Each bowed as he was introduced and the child giggled, then winced, but it was evident that no lasting damage had been done.

"You were clutching some flowers when I picked you up. Were they for your mama?"

"Yes, cos I thought they were pretty like she is."

Diana looked embarrassed. "Yes, well, thank you but I think them prettier. Now, I believe it's time we asked Uncle Gideon to carry you to your room, for I'm sure that a sleep will cure you of your headache."

He picked her up, nuzzling her neck as he did so and making her laugh. No-one spoke until he returned a few minutes later, but Diana urged them all to sit down.

"I must thank you all for coming so quickly to my rescue, but perhaps an explanation is in order."

Freddie and Thomas each waved a hand to indicate that none was necessary, but she continued.

"I don't know how much you have been told of my sorry tale, but I must assure you that Gideon is not the cause of my woe but my rescuer. Had it not been for him, I dread even to imagine where I and my child might be today. You might think I should not have accepted his charity."

"Now, that's enough, Diana. We have been through this before. I was in the fortunate position to be able to help and I wish to hear no more about it."

"That's all very well, but I wouldn't have your friends believe I took such advantage of your generosity."

It was Freddie's turn to interrupt. "Well, I've known him a long time now, and it's my opinion that once his mind is set upon something he will cast all obstacles aside to achieve his end."

Diana smiled. "Yes, it was pretty much like that. He is a difficult man to say no to."

"Well, I'm glad you know that much at least, for I am now going to tell you to sit with your daughter and relax when you can. You have had a very worrying day, but the outcome at least has been a good one. I will come and visit you again tomorrow, to see how Bella is progressing." He flicked her chin. "Don't worry, child. I feel certain she will have suffered no more than a few bruises, and look what an adventure she has had. She will be able to tell her friends all about it. Gentlemen?" he said, moving to hold the door open for them to pass through before him, but Thomas still had something to say.

"Perhaps I too may be permitted to call upon you, to see how Bella is, of course."

Diana blushed and Gideon smiled inwardly. Thomas visited Combe three times more before Patience returned to Bath.

Patience began making enquiries immediately and was saddened and horrified to learn that she would never in one lifetime be able to help all those in need. Accepting the facts as they were, where able she visited those women who were brought to her attention. Most were living in unimaginable squalor and came from all walks of Society, the majority being amongst the poorest but one or two more gently born. Each one had a story to tell. There were those for whom promiscuity had become a way of life. "How else can I put food in my babe's mouth, miss?" was a cry she heard more than once. She had no answer for them. Even disregarding the defensiveness of some, it was evident that most had been taken the grossest advantage of. One had been 'sold' by her mother to pay for food for a younger sibling. Would this be the fate of a child of one of these poor girls? Men had made promises.

"He told me he loved me. That we would be married when next he returned to Bath. I never saw him again."

"He raped me, miss. So strong he was, I had no chance."

"Such beautiful honest eyes he had, but they hid behind them a liar."

The stories were endless, the outcome always the same. But she wasn't a rich woman. Without funds of her own she had no choice but to appeal to others, but her mission might not be theirs. It would be necessary to proceed slowly, no matter how urgent was the problem. Being to a large extent realistic and acknowledging that she could not save them all, Patience chose six and heartbreakingly left the others to fend for themselves, not daring to give them hope by making promises she might not be able to fulfil. For the rest, she could at least provide sufficient sustenance that they might not starve.

It was her ambition to locate a house away from the city which could house all six women and their children, perhaps where they might keep a goat and some chickens, grow their own crops, become self-sufficient. It was a dream, but one that seemed attainable, if she could find someone to sponsor them until such time as they could manage on their own. She turned for help to her cousin Gideon, hiring a carriage to drive her to Worthington Place. She stopped first at the gatehouse to see Mary.

"What a delightful surprise, my dear. I thought you were still in Oakenchurch."

"No, I returned some days ago and have been busy ever since. But more of that later. How are you, my friend? I am certain this life suits you, for you are positively blooming."

"I have never been so happy in my life. I thought at first I would feel the lack of company, but the only one I miss is you. Hester comes practically every day and is much improved. I feel sure you will hardly recognise her. Then there is the gardener and the cook, who frequently brings delicious delights to me himself, as if I cannot cook," she chuckled. "And being right here by the entrance, I am able to view all the comings and goings to the big house. Mr Hildebrand and Mr Mulberry hardly ever go by without passing the time of day with me. As for your cousin, I think I have never met a kinder gentleman."

Patience felt a sudden pang. She was delighted for her friend, of course, and it was gone almost before it came, but she had recognised it and was disappointed in herself. Envy was not a quality of which she was proud. "Are you busy, Mary, or will you walk with me to the Place?"

"I could never be too busy for you. Give me a moment to fetch my shawl. Will you leave the carriage here?"

"I shall, for it is hired for the day. Abigail would have it that I shouldn't come alone but I could see no harm, knowing you would be here to watch over me."

"As if you needed that in your cousin's house."

They walked slowly, Mary taking up most of the conversation and informing Patience excitedly that she had received two more commissions but recently and didn't know how she was going to contrive to fulfil all her obligations.

"I can see I have no need in the slightest to be worried for you."

"Indeed no, but what of you, my dear?"

Fortunately they had by this time reached Worthington Place and Patience had no need to reply, other than to say, "Oh, I am well enough and I have several plans. I shall not bore you with them now."

All three men were in the drawing room with Hester, and the delight of each was apparent as she and Mary entered.

"My dearest cousin, it seems an age since we have had the pleasure of seeing you here."

Patience straightened up from where she had bent to embrace her aunt and took Gideon's hand, smiling warmly at him. "I was away from Bath for a week and have been busy since my return, but I could not allow another day to go by before coming to see Hester and to catch up on all the news. Thank you for your note, Thomas," she said, turning to him. "I am sorry I was not at home when you called, but I'm so pleased that you advised me of your intentions. And you, Freddie, have you got over your visit home? Was your sister well?"

Everyone laughed. He had made no secret of the antipathy between himself and his sibling.

"We contrived not to distress our parents too much by quarrelling in front of them, but I must say I was glad to get away. Tell us, if you will, what is all this busyness you have been up to?"

Patience demurred, instead expressing a desire to speak privately with her cousin.

"Would you care then to join me in the library, or may I first offer you some refreshment?"

"Tea would be wonderful, if you please, Gideon, but afterwards, yes, I do have something I wish to discuss with you."

CHAPTER NINETEEN

Once in the library, Patience found herself unsure as to where to begin. It wasn't that she didn't consider a gentleman's home to be a suitable place for such a discussion, but she had been so swept along by her own enthusiasm thus far that she needed a few moments to collect her thoughts.

"You are looking pensive, cousin. Is this something you would perhaps prefer to defer to another time?"

She marvelled at how he could read her so well, for she had considered herself to be at least outwardly calm.

"No, indeed. You must think me very foolish, but the subject I wish to discuss with you is a sensitive one."

"Then I suggest you sit down and take your time. Are you in a hurry to return to Bath?" he asked, for the moment turning the subject. "I know Mama would be delighted if you could remain with us for a few days."

Patience was grateful to Gideon for giving her time to compose herself. "I fear I must, if for no other reason than that of my wardrobe."

"Could what you require not be sent for?"

She was tempted, that much was certain, but she considered there to be occasions when temptation must be resisted and this was perhaps one of them. Who knew how he would receive what she had to say to him? "Another time, perhaps, and now I am ready to impart what I came to say." She folded her hands in her lap and looked directly into his warm brown eyes, distracted for a moment by the depth of colour she saw there. "When first I came here, it may be that I was somewhat brittle in my manner, particularly in the light of your proffered kindness to one who was, after all, a stranger."

Gideon's face displayed a smile of unholy amusement. "Brittle? You, my dear cousin?"

"Don't laugh at me. I have apologised, have I not?"

"Not, I think, but we shall pass over that. Do pray continue."

It was difficult to be serious when she could enjoy the joke as much as he. "Then I shall do so now. The point is, it was my first time away from home, and without my father. I was acutely apprehensive."

"You hid it well."

He really wasn't helping.

"I came to realise very speedily that I was of an independent mind. My rejection may have seemed churlish at the time. It came from the best of motives, I assure you."

"I am suitably reassured. Do go on."

She paused again, but it was time. "It has been some months now, and I have discovered in myself a need to find a direction. To do something useful. If only I had been born a man."

"Thank God you were not!" he said explosively.

"I beg your pardon?"

"You are, my dear cousin, sufficiently formidable as a woman."

"I shall take that as a compliment."

Good heavens, were they flirting with each other? Surely not. Patience got back to the business in hand.

"I was kneeling at my mother's graveside when an idea came to me, for I had been wondering what her fate might have been had my father not come to her rescue. Yes, I know, this is a delicate subject between the two of us, but I am not one to hide from the truth. Mama's behaviour was not what might have been expected from one so gently nurtured, but what of those young women who find themselves in impossible circumstances through no fault of their own? I decided upon my return to Bath to see what I could discover of those who were not fortunate enough to have a Nicholas Worthington in their lives. Sadly I have found many. Girls who are living an existence I would wish upon no-one, trying to support a child born out of wedlock and shunned by their families."

She paused, for Gideon's expression had changed entirely. He was looking decidedly grim. Yes, what she had described was grim, but this was more than that. Did he look angry? Her own features lost their previous animation and she said coolly, "You do not approve. I am sorry. I had hoped… But I see I can count you amongst those who believe that young women bring this fate upon themselves. I shall not mention it again. Perhaps we should join the others, and I can take my leave of my aunt."

Gideon, who had at first thought she had somehow learned of Diana's circumstances, realised his mistake almost immediately and strove to reassure her. "You misunderstand. If I appear angry, it is with the men who are the perpetrators, not their unfortunate victims. Do go on. Tell me what it is you have in mind."

Patience, greatly relieved, sat again on the chair she had suddenly vacated and continued. "It is obvious even to me —" and here she paused to smile — "that I cannot save the world. I have visited several girls and chosen six to aid if I can. For the moment I am supplying them with food, but it is little enough in the circumstances. You are aware that my own situation doesn't allow me to do much in the way of financial support."

She stood again, pacing up and down, a mixture of agitation and enthusiasm driving her, and Gideon had a few moments to observe her at his leisure. He thought her magnificent.

"My wish is to find a small farm with a house that they can share. Once it is established, it shouldn't be beyond possible for them to grow their own food and, with a little husbandry on the side, to supply milk and meat. Six women. Six children. They could live together in harmony without being spat upon in the street. Yes, sir, I assure you it happens. Only I do not have the funds for such an enterprise. I am looking for a sponsor."

She looked at him with fire and hope in her eyes. He was not proof against them. Besides, he had personal experience of such redemption. "And you have come to me. I am flattered."

His tone was unreadable, his expression also. The fire left her eyes and her shoulders sagged. She believed he was refusing her.

"This is a much larger project than perhaps you realise and will take further discussion, but I can see how it could work. Let us return to the others. In spite of the obvious urgency, we need to think this through carefully. But yes, I believe I can be of assistance."

Patience preceded Gideon to the drawing room, light of foot and even lighter of heart. She'd not thought beyond today, hoping fervently that he would fall in with her plans, not able to contemplate to whom she might go next if he refused her. He had the means, but did he have the will? It seemed he did.

"Aunt Hester, you must forgive me for such a fleeting visit, but I need to return home. So good, though, to see both you and Mary looking so well."

"Perhaps next time you might stay for a few days, while the weather still remains fine."

Patience said she would be delighted to do so and took her leave of Freddie and Thomas, both of whom promised to visit her in Bath. Her host walked with her to the gatehouse and repeated his mother's invitation as he handed her into the carriage.

"Nothing would give me greater pleasure, but I fear I must for the moment remain in Lansdown Crescent. Now that I have begun providing provisions for my girls —" how easily the expression tripped off her tongue — "I cannot all at once desert them."

"I can see your reasoning. I shall visit you tomorrow, if I may, so that we can discuss your project in more detail, but fear not, cousin. Already an idea has occurred to me, but I must consider it carefully before imparting it to you, for I should hate to disappoint you should it not prove viable. Certainly it would be good to get something in place as soon as possible, if only so that my mother does not fear you are rejecting her by not coming to stay."

"Oh no, pray reassure her. Nothing could be further from the truth."

"I was joking, Patience. Don't worry. We shall come about. Until tomorrow, then," he said, kissing her fingertips before letting go her hand and leaving her to sink back against the cushions in some confusion.

Arriving back at Lansdown Crescent a while later, her mind was not grappling with the problem in hand but dwelling on the sensation she had experienced when taking her leave of Gideon. When Abigail asked if she'd had an enjoyable time, she appeared to be so distracted that her companion feared she had met with failure, for while Patience had not told her exactly what she planned to say (she hardly knew herself) she was aware that she had intended to raise the subject of what she called the lost girls. Looking startled for a moment, Patience pulled her wits together and said, "Thank you, yes, very pleasant. My aunt is well, Mary is well, and my cousin visits tomorrow to discuss how we may proceed." She became animated once more. "Lord Lacey will help us, I think, Abigail. He mentioned that he had an idea. I could see a plan was formulating, but he wanted to be clear in his own mind before we talked about it. I wonder, would you mind tomorrow taking my maid and distributing the parcels that will have been prepared in the kitchen? I should hate to be absent when he arrives and, as he didn't indicate a time to me, I would like to remain at home in anticipation of his arrival."

"Certainly, and any other errand you might wish to charge me with. I must tell you that a gentleman called to see you while you were out. A Mr Dysart. He left his compliments and said he would come again another time. Whatever is wrong? You seem to be quite put out," she remarked, noticing the flicker of impatience that Patience exhibited. She hadn't seen him since before her visit to Oakenchurch. Not since he'd attempted to force himself upon her. She shuddered, remembering how grateful she'd been when Freddie had arrived so fortuitously.

"It's nothing. Just that I had hoped I had managed to shake him off. Doesn't that sound awful? But I must tell you that he has been rather particular in his attentions, and I believed I'd made it clear they were unwelcome. It seems I was wrong."

Patience waited for Gideon's visit the next day with far more eagerness than she liked to admit to herself, and the thought of working with him to find a solution for her girls was not the only reason. Had he been flirting with her yesterday? Were his feelings for her more than familial? She thrust the thought aside. It would not do to be dwelling on such things when there was a job to be done. He arrived in due course, and Freddie Hildebrand with him.

"I am come to pay my respects, having business in town which requires my attention. I shall return later and travel back to Worthington Place with Lacey. I must tell you that I shall soon be taking my leave of you all, my sister having departed the family home and duty calling me in the form of my father."

"I shall miss you, Freddie. Do you go soon?"

"Within a few days. The old gentleman is wishful to discuss estate matters, me being his heir an' all. My uncle popping off like that put the fear in him, I think, though he's much younger and should live for many more years. I hope so. Like him."

"Off you go now, Freddie, for Patience and I have much to discuss."

"Yes, of course. Great idea you have there, if I may be permitted to say so. Gideon told me a little about it. You couldn't have picked a better man to approach."

Gideon threw a quick irritated glance at his friend, which went completely over his head but was intercepted by Miss Worthington. *Now what on earth has Freddie said to annoy him so?* she wondered. He looked at her again, and the smile had returned.

Ringing for tea, she sat down and he sat opposite. She asked him to make known to her the idea that he had alluded to the previous day.

"A simple one, to all intents and purposes. You have in the past ridden my land with me and must be aware that it is extensive. There are several tenant farmers and I had only to cast my mind about to see if any such property was at present vacant."

"And?" Her excitement was tangible.

"And there are two which are at present unoccupied. It occurs to me that you might like to inspect them to judge which you think more suitable. You could remain for a few days, thus gratifying my mother's wish to spend time with you." He held up his hand against the interruption which was so evidently coming. "I have already anticipated your objection, but surely arrangements can be made in your absence for sustenance to be provided. We must be sure to make the right decision, for the future of these people is at stake."

"It will be some considerable time before they become established sufficiently to pay you rent. You will, in the meantime, be losing income."

Gideon berated her for insulting him and sent her a look so cold that she shivered. He was, he assured her, able to bear the loss indefinitely, and if this venture was to be a success she must cease being ingenuous and behave like an adult. She rather liked this side of him, though she was at pains not to let it show. Instead, she assured him that she could leave Abigail in Bath to deal with the practical side of providing supplies, she herself needing no chaperon other than her aunt.

"Then it is arranged. I shall collect you tomorrow. Thunderbolt will, I am certain, enjoy the company when we ride out the following day," he said with a smile that warmed her heart.

The smile fled a moment later when the door was opened and the footman announced, "Mr Dysart, miss."

A scowl distorted Gideon's features, a similar expression crossing the other man's face. Dysart was the quicker to recover. "Good day to you. It is an age since last we met, but it seems I have chosen an unfortunate moment to visit."

"My cousin and I have been discussing a business matter, sir."

"In that case, I shall take my leave of you and hope to see you again soon, perhaps in the Pump Room." He bowed himself out again.

Patience turned to find such a look of anger on Gideon's face as to frighten her a little.

"Have I not told you to avoid that man? Nothing good can come of you associating with him."

It was her turn to be outraged, and she told him in no uncertain terms that he was not her keeper and until he gave her a reason for warning her so, she would associate with whomsoever she pleased. They were still arguing when Freddie walked into the room, exclaiming, "Was that Dysart I just saw walking down the street? The cheek of the man. After what happened the last time, I should have thought he would have abandoned his pursuit of you. I should send him packing if I were you."

"Just what I've been telling her, Freddie," Gideon said through gritted teeth, the spitfire beside him striving also to control her emotions. "It is time we too were leaving. I shall see you tomorrow as arranged, cousin." There was no hiding the steel in his voice, and the door had no sooner closed behind them than she burst into tears.

Patience would have given much to know the cause of her cousin's antipathy and had silently berated herself for not telling her footman to refuse Dysart, should he come calling. She had remedied the omission immediately and then, pent-up energy giving her frustration no outlet, she walked to Upper Camden Place at such a pace that her maid had difficulty keeping up with her. Fortunately for her, Clara was home. She was greeted with enthusiasm and the boys were sent off to the schoolroom, for Mrs Buxton could tell immediately that this was no ordinary call.

"Whatever is the matter, dearest? You look as if you have received terrible news."

"No, nothing as dreadful as that." She drew off her gloves and emitted a half-hearted laugh. "I have once again quarrelled with my cousin."

"But I thought all was now well between you?"

"And so did I, and it was." Patience went on to relate the circumstances of the previous few hours and included what she had not told Clara before, about Dysart's molesting her in her own drawing room. She received as much sympathy as she could have wished, a reprimand for having been so lax as to forget to bar the aggressor from the house and a curiosity that matched her own as to what lay between the two men.

"And tomorrow he comes to take me to Worthington Place for a few days. You may imagine how much I'm anticipating that now."

"Yes. Awkward. Could you not make your excuses and go another time?"

Patience leaned forward in her chair, her eyes glistening and her whole attitude altered as she poured the story of the project into Clara's willing ears. Mrs Buxton was at first a little shocked to think that her cousin was mixing with young women in such circumstances. One raised eyebrow, though, brought her to her senses and she was filled with admiration for her selflessness and dedication to others, suspecting there was more of Nicholas Worthington in his daughter than she had previously appreciated. The plan as presented to her seemed an admirable one, the only fault being that the benefactor was Lord Lacey. Though she admired him greatly, it was unfortunate that things stood as they did between Patience and Gideon, for such a venture would doubtless require close association.

"Will you be able to work together, do you think?"

"We must, Clara, for the fate of twelve people depends upon us doing so."

"Then you must treat each other as business partners and put your personal feelings aside."

The trouble was, Patience didn't know what her personal feelings were. One moment there seemed to be a connection between her and Gideon such that no words were required. At other times, though, the words spoken between them were as polite strangers.

The walk into town and home again settled her and, instead of passing a sleepless night as she'd expected, she rose the next morning filled with eager anticipation but also with dread.

Gideon came as promised, but there was no doubting the coolness between them. They were as civil acquaintances and Patience, having taken her leave of Abigail, could almost have wished she had remained in Bath. But this wasn't about her, so instead of raising the subject of Jasper Dysart again, which was what she wanted to do, she answered him politely but with distance.

"My mother is looking forward to your visit, and I make no doubt Mary will enjoy spending time with you again."

The words were all they should have been, but they were spoken as stiffly as the man from whom they emanated. Patience replied in kind, expressing her gratitude and her pleasure at having an opportunity to see Freddie before his departure, and also Thomas Mulberry, whom she knew still to be at Worthington Place. A nod of the head was all the acknowledgement she received, but she decided to attribute this to his concentration on driving.

"And have you informed my aunt of our plans?"

"No, for I thought it was something we ought to do together. In any case, we should wait until we have verified the suitability of the premises I have in mind."

Patience, unable or at least unwilling to deal with Gideon if this rift between them was to continue, felt forced to say, "If we are destined to remain at loggerheads, cousin, do you not consider that perhaps we should abandon the scheme altogether?"

He, astonished at such forthrightness, allowed his concentration to drop for a moment and with it the reins. One of the horses stumbled and he gathered his team together before replying with an edge to his voice, "Surely we can rise above our differences to aid these poor young women. I did not think you would abandon them so readily. Or are you of the opinion that you might easily find another benefactor?"

Hostility hung between them.

"I am not, and as far as I can tell there is only the one difference between us, which might easily be resolved if you would but give me a reason for cautioning me."

"Well, I'm afraid you have me there. The honour of one other than myself is at stake and I will not betray a confidence, even for you, cousin. If you cannot accept that, I am sorry, but I will not change my mind."

"Then it only remains for me to hope that we may continue in the manner of business partners. I understand that men sometimes have an exaggerated sense of honour, but you must also appreciate that I do not bow to another's will without good reason."

"There is very good reason."

"Perhaps, but without knowledge I cannot act upon it. We must in this case agree to differ."

"And I must sincerely hope that you do not come to grief because of your obduracy."

The remainder of the journey passed in silence.

CHAPTER TWENTY

Patience was disappointed to find Thomas absent when they arrived at Worthington Place, for he had a manner which immediately set all in his presence at their ease. She need not have worried, though, because Freddie had the same affability. In any case, Gideon would not allow their disagreement to show in front of his mother. Just acting the part enabled both him and Patience to relax, and by the time greetings had been exchanged the atmosphere was slightly less chilly. Sufficiently so for Gideon to take her into the library and spread open a map of the estate to show her the position of the properties he had in mind.

"Yes, I can follow your thinking. Both are sufficiently distanced from others to enable their occupants to lead secluded lives, should they choose to do so, but close enough to engage with the neighbours if that is desirable. It is to be hoped that with the passing of time, they may engage with your tenants and build friendships away from the house, but they will not be thrust into the company of others if they do not wish to be." She looked up at him and was rewarded with the glimmer of a smile. "It can work can't it, Gideon? I cannot tell you how grateful I am to you."

"You have nothing to be grateful for. It makes my blood boil to think of these girls being so taken advantage of and believe me, it doesn't only happen amongst the poorer classes."

He spoke with a passion that suggested he was more than merely an interested bystander, but because she was so at one with him in this sentiment she didn't pause to consider his comment pointed in any way. Freddie knocked on the door and said that Tom had returned, and they were off to spend the rest of the day fishing.

"He's just changing his clothes. I didn't like to interrupt you, but I thought I'd check if you wanted to join us, Gideon?"

"What do you say, cousin? Do you fancy a bit of fishing?"

"Thank you, no. Do go, by all means, and I shall spend the time with Hester and Mary. I think we've finished here for the moment, don't you? I look forward to going to see the houses properly tomorrow."

"Discussing the properties, are you?" Freddie went to have a look at the plan and, having a fair knowledge of the estate, was able to add his approval to that of Patience. "I see they lie in the same direction as Combe. That's convenient."

"Combe? Is that also on your land?"

"No, just beyond. A small village only, but one that I've had reason to visit occasionally."

Patience might have thought nothing of the exchange except for the look that passed from Gideon to Freddie, which she could not interpret at all. There was no time for her to wonder about it, though, as her cousin once more rolled up the map and Freddie held the door for her to pass out of the room. Mary had arrived in her absence and was sitting with Hester. The gentlemen left and she didn't see Thomas at all until they sat down to dine some hours later, and she was only able to have a quiet word with him some time after that.

"I was sorry to have missed you earlier, Thomas. Do you have friends in the neighbourhood?"

"Someone I have met only recently. I must tell you," he continued, looking more than a little self-conscious, "that I have been to visit her nearly every day."

"Her?" Patience smiled encouragingly.

"She lives quietly. I can assure you I have been at pains not to be alone with her or to compromise her in any way. I believe I have lost my heart, Patience."

"I am more than happy to hear so, my friend. And will I be able to meet her soon, your young lady?"

For the first time he appeared to be uncomfortable and did not look at her directly. She was surprised, for what could there be to make him reticent? Nothing untoward, she hoped.

"Her circumstances are a little unusual. I hope, in time, when I know her better, that is … but for now I must not break a confidence."

More secrets? thought Patience.

"But I'm glad to have had this opportunity to see you this evening, Patience, for I shall be off to Combe again tomorrow. Ah, here are Lacey and Hildebrand, returned from escorting Mary to the gatehouse. And don't you believe a word either of them said earlier, for I can assure you mine was the biggest catch of the day."

Everyone laughed, but Patience had picked up on something Thomas had said. Had he not mentioned Combe? Was that not the place Gideon and Freddie had been so enigmatic about in the library?

The next day, all four left Worthington Place on horseback together, Freddie having expressed an interest in joining Patience and Gideon and Thomas; the latter would ride with them before veering off in the direction of Combe. It turned out to be a good thing, because it was difficult for anyone to be at outs in Freddie's company. With Patience eager to view the properties and Gideon anxious to see if either or both met with her approval, the atmosphere between the cousins was much lighter than on the previous day

Having enjoyed a good gallop, they tethered the horses outside the first and entered what was quite a substantial building to find dust lying everywhere, it not having been occupied for some considerable time. No curtains hung on the windows and no furniture graced the rooms, but Patience could see the potential in a space that offered sufficient bedrooms if each child shared with its mother. The kitchen and living area were spacious and two further rooms were found to adjoin them on the ground floor. In the far corner of one was an old spinning wheel, covered in cobwebs, the only piece of furniture in the whole place, but it made Patience think that this might be another occupation to be considered.

As they moved through the back door to the rear of the house she, brushing some gossamer from her skirt as she went, could see that there was more than enough land to accommodate what she had envisaged. The garden was overgrown, but there were remnants of what had once been a vegetable patch. There would be room and more for chickens, definitely a pig, a cow and perhaps some goats in the field beyond. Perhaps, thinking of the spinning wheel she'd seen inside, even some sheep. She tried not to be overly excited, but her eyes were glistening as she turned to Gideon and said, "It's perfect, cousin."

The last of his anger at her abated as he saw her enthusiasm. This was not some lady of fashion who thought only of what gown she might wear or which play she would enjoy. Here was a woman of substance who would take on any challenge and meet it with courage. Had she not already done so, having been left in circumstances that might have daunted many others in her position? He laughed. "Well, Hildebrand, it would seem my choice has met with some approval. What do you think?"

"Excellent, and when I think what Diana has made of the place you set up for her, well, there's as much potential here for certain."

"Diana?" Patience asked, for the context was questionable to say the least. The look that passed between the two men was the same as she had seen yesterday, but Gideon merely said, "A friend who needed help."

To enquire further would have been rude, but there was no doubt her curiosity was piqued. Instead, she asked if they might now visit the second site. She found it to be as satisfactory as the first, the configuration being slightly different but in essence it carried with it the same potential. Declaring that she could not choose between the two, she was surprised to hear Freddie say, "Use 'em both. Why not? I'm sure it won't be difficult to find occupants."

"Exactly what I was thinking, but I would suggest that we begin with one, my cousin here already having the first young women ready to act when she gives the word. What do you say, Patience? We can leave the second unoccupied for the time being and concentrate on the first."

She had become quiet, he knew not for what reason, but when she looked up at him he could see that she appeared to be disturbed.

"Is something wrong?"

There was indeed something wrong. She had realised that as willing as they might be to work, there was no way the girls could move into either building in their present state. A considerable sum would have to be expended to put things in order, for furniture to be supplied, for the house to be equipped. Even if they were to make their own curtains, they would need a chair to sit on. A bed to sleep in. She looked acutely embarrassed as she explained what was troubling her.

"I cannot pay for such things. It is all very well to accept from you the occupancy of buildings that are standing empty, but to expect you to expend money to refurbish them? It is foolish of me, but I hadn't anticipated it. I fear I shall have to abandon the project, for this is something I cannot ask of you."

"You have not asked, and I am happy to provide whatever is needed. You must surely know by now that my sentiments on this subject are the same as yours."

"Yes, for have you not already done something similar for your friend Diana?"

All at once the atmosphere was cold again. How could she have been so gauche as to ask such a question?

"What I have or have not done for Diana is none of your business. I suggest we ride back to Worthington Place now, and you may compile a list of such things as you think will be required to put the first house in order. I imagine it will take some time, and the sooner we can get this finalised the better. In the meantime, I shall arrange to have the property cleaned from top to bottom in preparation for what is to come."

They rode in silence, but the one who felt most wretched was Freddie, for it was he who had set the cat amongst the pigeons.

Patience was walking later in the day in the shrubbery at the back of the house. She needed time away from her cousin, for it seemed they could not meet without falling into some disagreement or other. It gave her time too to think back over what had been said and what interpretation she might put upon it. Thomas came looking for her. She was glad of his company, for she seemed to be going around in circles.

"I trust you have had a pleasant day, sir," she said, smiling warmly at him, as ever relaxed in his company.

"Never better. May I join you on your walk? We have barely seen each other and I have only a short time ago returned from Combe."

Combe again, Patience thought. "Is that not where your young lady resides?"

Thomas laughed. "I hardly think she would consider 'resides' as being an appropriate word, for it suggests something grander, in my mind at least, than the humble cottage in which she lives with her daughter."

"She has a child, then?"

"Yes. Bella. A delightful four-year-old whom I have had the pleasure of entertaining today by setting her on the back of my horse and walking her up and down the lane."

"Is she widowed then, the lady?"

"No, she has never been married. It was lucky for her after the birth of her child that Gideon settled her as he did. She is grateful to him, for he has watched over her ever since. It's how I met her, in fact, for he was going there one day and Freddie and I were permitted to accompany him. They are great friends nowadays and he visits often."

Patience was more shocked than she could say and made no comment at all initially, but her thoughts were riotous. She was aware that men regarded the world in an entirely different way to women and that liaisons were not uncommon and often held quite openly. But for Gideon to set up his mistress or, as Thomas had suggested, his erstwhile mistress, so close to home and then introduce her to his friends? It would appear from the little that had been said that she was of gentle birth. Why had he not made an honest woman of her? And a child too!

She felt contempt and disappointment, unsure which sentiment was uppermost but enjoying neither.

"Is her name Diana?"

"Yes, how did you know? I haven't asked her yet because we have only been acquainted a short while, but I can tell you, Patience, that it is my dearest hope that she will become my wife."

"Something Freddie and Gideon were saying when we visited the proposed sanctuaries earlier today," she said in reply to his question. "I hope your wish is granted, my friend, for I desire nothing more than to see you happy."

"Well, I do not despair, for she greets me every day with a smile and seems happy for me to play with Bella. I am surprised, though, that she was mentioned in your presence, for Gideon has all this time kept her away from the world and safe. It was only a happy chance that I met her at all, for her child had gone missing on a day that Hildebrand and I were with him. She sent him a note, begging for him to come and help in the search, and it was urgent enough that he didn't fob us off but allowed us to accompany him. In fact, it was I who found Bella."

He rambled on in this style, but all Patience could think was that Gideon had provided for his mistress and her child but that he had withheld his guilty secret from his friends. From everyone. He had not done the honourable thing and married her. She considered him contemptible and could not wait to leave Worthington Place for fear of betraying her disgust and Thomas's trust. Hester and Mary both expressed their disappointment when, upon returning to the house, she announced her intention of returning to Bath the next day.

"But my dear, you have only just arrived."

"I know, but after viewing the houses yesterday I cannot wait to tell the girls what is in store for them and to purchase some material so that they may begin making curtains. It will mean so much to them, don't you see? Give them hope and perhaps some pride and, most of all, a goal. For the first time since their misery began, they will be able to look to their future. It would be selfish of me to remain here when I have such important news to impart to them, but I hope you will allow me to come again, Aunt Hester, at some later date."

It was a reasonable excuse and none found fault with it. She took her leave the next day, receiving a hug from Freddie. "I shall be leaving too and know not when we shall meet again, Patience," he said.

Patience fought back the tears, told Thomas she hoped to see him soon and thanked her cousin coolly as he handed her into the carriage.

"I shall put in motion those things we discussed and let you know when it will be convenient to organise transport for your protégées to their new home. Do not worry, Patience. Together we shall make this happen."

Men! Would she ever understand them?

Abigail accepted without question the reason for Patience's early return to Lansdown Crescent, and they went the following day to a delightful warehouse where they purchased sufficient material to cover six bedroom windows, each of a different pattern, together with such needles and threads as might be required. All having been divided into the requisite number of parcels, they then visited the girls in turn and Patience could barely hold back a tear at the excitement as every one of them exclaimed eagerly, keen to begin their tasks immediately.

"I cannot at this time give you a firm date for your removal from Bath, but I promise you it will not be long. There are preparations to be made, but if all goes well you should be in your new home before winter sets in." This she told them all, one only, Gladys by name, shifting uncomfortably from one foot to the other.

"Is something troubling you, my dear?" Patience asked.

Gladys shuffled again before taking a deep breath as if to make a confession. "I ain't never learned to sew, miss. Me ma ran when I were just a kid and Dad, well, if I ever saw 'im sober I don't recall. There weren't no-one to show me how."

Patience was for a moment nonplussed, but it was Abigail who said, "Then I wonder if we should find some place where you could all meet for a while every day. You could help each other. You are, after all, going to be living together, so I see no reason why you shouldn't first become acquainted."

"An excellent idea. I shall visit the vicar. I would be surprised if he did not know of some such place."

"I ain't no churchgoer, miss. Never been in my life."

"Well, it's never too late to begin. In any case, I am not asking you to pray but to sew. Now, don't worry anymore. We'll soon have you setting your stitches and maybe in time you might even be able to make clothes for you and your little one."

"That would make a change from stealing them, that's for sure," Gladys said with a grin the other two could not help responding to. They were under no illusions.

After this episode, Patience was more determined than ever to remove the girls to a safer environment, and others after them if she could. For this reason, she resolved to put to the back of her mind those censorious thoughts she had about Gideon and to work with him as best she could to achieve her goal. He was surprised, therefore, when she sent a message a few days later asking if she might return to Worthington Place to see her aunt. This time, as they drove back, their talk was of their scheme. She was delighted to learn that work had already begun and Gideon promised to take her to inspect progress at the first opportunity.

"My mother, I know, is anxious to spend some time with you, but perhaps we might resume our rides and combine the two."

Her eyes were glistening, though he could not see, concentrating as he was on his driving. She found herself wishing it could always be thus with them, for when they were in accord there was none with whom she felt more comfortable.

Hester was undoubtedly pleased to see her, eager to show her the results of her labours. "I must tell you that since Mary's arrival I have once more taken up my brushes. You will be aware that she purchased some new ones for me and a box of paints. We spend much of our time in companionable silence, in the garden mostly, though I have set aside a room where we may both occupy ourselves to our hearts' content and the light in there is excellent. She has taken to coming here rather than subjecting me to going to the gatehouse. Although I was enjoying it, I also found it quite exhausting and prefer to expend what little energy I have on painting. You will think me foolish, I expect."

"Not at all. I could not be more delighted that you have rediscovered something so dear to your heart. Is Mary not here now?"

"She will arrive shortly, I am sure. Now, tell me about these girls of yours. Gideon seems very keen on the project, and I think it an undertaking which is a credit to you both."

Patience told her about Gladys, and she sighed and she smiled in equal measure, exclaiming that if all were so characterful it should become a lively household. Mary tripped into the room and embraced her friend. Patience could only think how well she looked and how contented. They talked of all manner of things and were surprised when they realised it was time to change for dinner.

"Thomas is still with us, as you can see," Gideon said as they sat down, "though he threatens to leave us soon."

"I fear I have traded too long upon your hospitality and must return to my family. It has been some weeks now, and there are things I wish to discuss with my father."

Patience looked enquiringly at him, but the dinner table was not the place for an exchange of confidences. She wondered if he had yet offered marriage to Diana and what had been her reply. He didn't look downhearted, so she could only assume that all was well and hoped that tomorrow would bring an opportunity to talk.

CHAPTER TWENTY-ONE

The next morning, Thomas joined Patience and Gideon as before when they set out to ride and once more left them to continue on to Combe. It seemed to Patience that all must therefore be progressing as he wished with Diana.

As Patience and Gideon approached the property they'd selected for their project, now renamed Hope Cottage, she forgot all about Thomas, for even as they came near she could see it bore little resemblance to what she had seen before. The small front garden had been cleared and the porch roof, which had before shown signs of falling to the ground, had been repaired. Climbing plants still remained on the front of the house, but their tendrils had been removed from the windows and it was a much brighter room that she entered.

"I cannot believe what has already been done, Gideon. You must have employed an army of men," she said, moving out of the way of one who was carrying some timber. She could hear also the noise of industry, unmistakably building work.

"We are fortunate that the property is on the whole sound, so much can be done simultaneously without awaiting reparations. I am happy you are pleased with it."

"Pleased! I am delighted and cannot wait to see their faces when we bring the girls here. Have you given any thought to the vegetable patch, or livestock?"

"I have. I will provide chickens and any other animals we deem suitable, but I'm wondering if we shouldn't leave the garden as it is. It wouldn't do to leave them with nothing to tackle, for I'm sure they will wish to get to work themselves,

With luck there will be sufficient time for them to prepare the land and plant winter vegetables. What do you think?"

Patience thought it an excellent idea and said so. They discussed also the prospect of each having differing skills. One might be happiest in the kitchen while another toiled the land and perhaps a third might best enjoy housewifely skills. It was something best left to them to sort for themselves, but by working together they should be able to establish a successful living. They rode back to Worthington Place in harmony, each secretly hoping it would continue.

Later that day, Thomas once more sought Patience in the shrubbery, having rightly concluded that it had become for her a place for solitude and contemplation.

"I trust I do not intrude, but I was wishful of speaking to you in private."

It was obvious he was big with news and she asked if he would like to sit on one of the benches or to walk.

"Walk, if you please, for I cannot be still. Diana has consented to become my wife. I am so happy I would shout it to the world, but first I must seek out my parents, for the circumstances are a little unusual. It would be unfair of me to make any announcement before consulting them."

"You need their permission?"

"Not at all but, as you are already aware, she has a child. There are no ties between Diana and her family. They have in the past treated her more shabbily than I can say."

Patience frowned, but whether from concern for Diana or disapproval of her parents Thomas could not tell.

"Things are not always as they appear, and people are only too ready to jump to conclusions. So you see, it is imperative that I tell my parents the true facts. I must look also for a place for us to live. It was time anyway that I left home." He laughed and his smiled broadened. "Naturally we cannot stay in Gideon's cottage, and I'm certain he will be more than delighted to be relieved of his responsibility, but I cannot tell him until I have returned from Mulberry Lodge."

Patience missed her step for a moment, more than ever surprised at how men could speak so freely of what was to her mind a distasteful situation. Thomas caught her elbow and they continued on their way. She could feel the happiness emanating from this man she was so pleased to call her friend and was hopeful that it would not be too long before she would be able to meet his chosen bride. Such was his adoration that it reminded her of the love her own parents had felt for each other, and she was anxious to know that Diana felt the same about him. Unwillingly the thought crept into her mind that here was an acceptable solution to the young mother's problem. She dismissed it, determined not to pre-judge in such a way as Thomas had suggested others had done before. She would wait until she knew what the unusual circumstances were that he had referred to, other than what she already knew. Her own mother's position had also been unusual. She hoped with all her heart that Thomas had found such a love as that between Lizzie and Nicholas Worthington.

"Then may I be the first to wish you happy, Thomas. When do you leave?"

"Tomorrow morning. Gideon is already aware that I was to go, so it will seem nothing out of the ordinary. I hope to return within a week or so, when it is my earnest wish that you will come with me to meet my betrothed."

He spoke with such pride and she answered in all truth, "I shall look forward to it, and to meeting Bella too."

"I hope I have not laid a burden upon you, Patience, but if I didn't tell somebody I think I might have burst."

They turned back to the house together, laughing as they went.

On the third day after Thomas's departure, Patience received a note. It was written in a hand she did not recognise — it certainly wasn't from Abigail. She placed it in her reticule and went as soon as she could to the shrubbery to read it in private. As well she did, for she gasped as she read its contents.

My dear Patience,

I hope you don't mind me using your given name but it is how Thomas refers to you, and as such it feels more natural to me. It will come as no surprise to you to learn that he has spoken of you often, for he values your friendship highly. It is my earnest wish that there should be no awkwardness between us, and it is for this reason I would ask you to visit me. You will understand why I cannot come to you. Please say nothing to Gideon. I have no secrets from him except this one, for I have promised Thomas I shall say nothing of our betrothal but, as he sent me a quick note before he left Worthington Place, I am aware that you are in possession of some of the facts. I would make the rest known to you if I may.

Hopefully,
Diana Painswick

Patience tried hard to think of a reason to leave without lying but also not betraying Diana's confidence. Fortune smiled upon her, because the next morning took Gideon to Bath on some errand and she was thus able to ride out alone. She took no-one with her, not even a groom, and having access to the map in the library was able to plan her route and arrived unflustered but filled with curiosity. She dismounted at the very pretty cottage and tied up her horse. There was a child playing in the front garden.

"Good morning. I am Patience, and you must be Bella. I have come to see your mama."

Two big blue eyes looked up at her from a face that in no way resembled Gideon. Is that what she had expected?

"I have my own patch in the garden. Can you see?" the child said, sweeping a chubby hand across to her left. "Mama did say she wasn't sure but that there might be a visitor. Is that you?"

"I hope so."

"Come then." Bella put her chubby, grubby hand into hers and led Patience towards the front door.

The door opened as they approached, and in its frame stood a beautiful young woman of a similar age to Patience. Her dark brown curls were pinned high on her head with one or two escaping the cap she wore to hold them in place. A look of such purity emanated from her, her smile so welcoming, that any pre-conceived idea her visitor may have had vanished in a flash. This was no loose-living woman. Nor did she bear any resemblance to the unfortunate girls Patience was at present seeking to help. Diana Painswick was a gentlewoman, of that there could be no doubt.

"I'm so glad you felt able to come. Do please join me inside. Bella, perhaps you might remain in the garden and pick some flowers for Miss Worthington."

"Are you married to Uncle Gideon? His name is Worthington, isn't it, Mama?"

"No, we are cousins," she replied, inwardly flustered but outwardly calm, "and yes please, flowers would be lovely."

When Patience entered the parlour, she felt she could have been standing in the drawing room of any home of any of her contemporaries. The curtains and furnishings were of chintz to match with the style of property, but everywhere was good taste.

"Do sit down, please, and I shall tell you why I asked you to come. How did you manage to get away from Gideon? He guards me so well that it is only recently he has brought anyone here in over four years. But you know that much already, I presume."

"I know very little other than that you are living, forgive me, under his protection."

"That's true, but not in the way you might imagine. I must take you back five years to when I lived in London, an innocent just making her debut. I do not deny that Gideon was one of my suitors but, knowing so little of the world, I was beguiled by one who had charm in abundance but who was lacking in principles. My parents too didn't recognise him for what he was and allowed us far more licence that was wise. I need not tell you what happened, for you have met my daughter. Mama and Papa, having failed in their duty to protect me, proceeded to disown me. Gideon and Jasper had been friends and…"

"Jasper! Dysart, do you mean?"

"Yes, it was Jasper Dysart who was the cause of my downfall, but it was your cousin who was my saviour. He had seen it all. Tried to warn me. Like the young fool I was I had put it down to jealousy and, what will you, an eighteen-year-old who thinks she's in love? Gideon challenged him to honour his obligations. He told me later that Jasper laughed in his face. I have never seen him since. You will think I should not have accepted Gideon's help, but I was desperate. He brought me to Combe, where I was confined, and here I have remained ever since. And though I would not have chosen the means of her conception, I thank the Lord for my daughter. She is the joy of my life."

Diana paused for a while to give Patience an opportunity to absorb what she had said, making the fetching of some lemonade an excuse for leaving the room for a few moments. Her head in a whirl, Patience realised she would have to revise her previous opinion. So that's why Gideon had tried so hard to warn her against Dysart. And what a foolish perception of ethics that then forbade him to explain why. No wonder Freddie had thought him up to the task of rescuing her girls. How could she so grossly have misjudged him? Her hostess returned with the promised refreshment and Patience drank thirstily, for her throat had suddenly become very dry.

"Pray continue, if you will."

"Gideon chose Combe, rather than somewhere on his own land, for he wanted to grant me anonymity, but he comes so often that those who live locally had their suspicions for a long while, until it became evident we were not lovers after all."

"And does he love you still?" Patience asked, suddenly breathless.

Diana laughed. "He regards me as a younger sister and bullies me sometimes, just as a brother would do."

Bella came in, clutching a bunch of wildflowers.

"Ah, Bella, thank you," her mother smiled. "They are very pretty. And now perhaps you might play in your room, for I wish to be private with Miss Worthington for a little longer."

"Yes, Mama."

Diana returned to her story as Bella left the room. "And then Gideon brought Thomas here, and this time I truly lost my heart. I could not believe it when he continued to visit. He knows everything and still he wants to marry me. He has gone to tell his parents of my situation. Not everything, of course, but the bare facts are irrefutable, and he would not consider deceiving them. Impossible, with Bella, but I might have pretended to be a widow. He would not hear of it. I pray the squire and his lady are as he has described them, and I honour him for his trust in them, but I must tell you, Patience, my heart flutters every time I think of what their reaction might be."

"Then allow me to reassure you, if I can. I have met Squire and Mrs Mulberry, and I have every faith that Thomas's confidence is not misplaced. I cannot say enough how happy I am for you both."

"And you can now see how misplaced were your imaginings about Gideon and me? There is no finer man walking this earth. Well, except for Thomas, of course. I hope we shall see much of each other in future, for I know he values your friendship above all others."

"And I hope you can forgive me, for in a world only too ready to assume the worst of people, I too was guilty."

"It is done. Let us say no more about it. Now, let me fetch Bella before you go, for she would be so disappointed not to say goodbye."

Patience rode home at a gentle pace, her thoughts far more occupied by what she had left behind than the journey back to Worthington Place. She could only hope she did not blush when she next met Gideon, for how could she not feel remorse that she had so misjudged him?

During the next few days, while she waited for Thomas to return, Patience found herself faced with a dilemma. Instinct screamed at her to apologise to Gideon, but she could not betray the confidence Diana had placed in her. Her cousin wasn't the only one with principles. If he noticed a softening in her attitude towards him, he did not remark upon it.

They continued to ride each day, inspecting progress at Hope Cottage as part of their routine, for such it had become. Gideon's trip to Bath, she learned, had been to procure furniture and those items as were required to equip the kitchen and the rest of the house. Her list, he told her, had come in very useful. "There are things that only a woman would think of. I also took the opportunity to purchase some toys for the children. I'm sure they will be able to make their own entertainment, but it won't hurt in the beginning to help them." Patience was once again brought to see what a kind and thoughtful man he was, and the now familiar constriction in her throat was once more in evidence. The livestock, he said, would be provided from his own estate when the time came, and that time would not be long in coming.

Thomas appeared one day at Worthington Place, and it was evident to Patience that his errand had prospered. Surely he could not look so happy if his parents had dissented. Still he said nothing, waiting only until the following morning to visit Diana and riding with Patience and Gideon part of the way as before. He waved them goodbye and they did not see him again until suppertime, when he said, "I should like you both to come with me to Combe tomorrow, if you will."

Gideon looked uncertain, for his mother had no knowledge of Diana's existence or proximity, but Thomas turned then to Hester and said, "You have been more than unusually kind to me, and I must tell you now that while I have been staying at Worthington Place I have been fortunate to meet a young lady. Perhaps you have noticed that I have been absent for many hours each day."

"Not at all. I dare say I wouldn't understand half the pursuits you young men undertake."

"This pursuit has been one which I hope you will understand and approve of. The lady has consented to be my wife. I have this past week been visiting with my parents to advise them of the situation and I come back with their blessing. Miss Painswick has requested that I bring Patience and Gideon to meet her before we remove, as we will do almost immediately, to my family home so that the banns may be read. We are anxious to be wed as soon as possible."

Gideon rose from his chair and went to where Thomas was sitting, first thumping him on his shoulder then wringing his hand with enthusiasm. "I could not be more happy for you, my dear friend. I shall be delighted to meet your betrothed," he said guardedly, not wishing to lie before his mother nor yet revealing that he was already acquainted with the bride-to-be. He'd seen it coming, of course, but that didn't make the news any less welcome. At last Diana had found the happiness she deserved. He was uncertain what part Patience played in all this, but the matter was now out of his hands.

He was astonished as they left next morning when Thomas turned to her and said, "Diana tells me she is so looking forward to seeing you again and how grateful she is that you complied with her request."

"You have met her!" Gideon exclaimed.

"Yes, Gideon, three days since. She asked that I go and see her. Told me the reason for Tom's journey." Patience paused. "Told me everything, in fact. I was sworn to secrecy until his return, so I have been unable until now to tell you how very much I honour you for what you have done."

Gideon reddened. "No such thing. It's only what any man would have done."

"No, not any man, and certainly not the one who was responsible for her situation. I understand now why you warned me about him. If only you could have been more open and told me why, we need not have been at outs so many times."

"I could not. It would not have been the act of a gentleman."

"I fear that is something upon which we shall never agree, but at least it is now in the open and will no longer stand as a barrier between us."

It was forthright of her, but it was something she felt needed to be said. Thomas took no part in the conversation but stared resolutely ahead. But he was smiling. He was still smiling when they reached Combe and Bella ran out of the cottage shouting excitedly, "Uncle Gideon, Uncle Gideon, Thomas is going to marry Mama. He has told me that after the wedding I may call him Papa. And we are going to meet *his* mama and papa, who will be my grandmama and grandpapa. I am SO excited."

Gideon swung her up in his arms and twirled her around, telling her she was a very lucky girl, but the smile he bestowed upon Diana was one of warmth and approval. "It would seem my work here is done."

She laughed and beckoned them all inside. "Not quite, my dearest friend, for I have one last favour to ask of you. I could not be wed without you there to support me as you have done all these years. It seems to me that it would be a fitting end to your guardianship if you were to give me away. And you, Patience. I have no family to stand by me. I would ask you to fulfil that role, for even though we have met but once it is my earnest hope that we will become great friends. We are to be married at the local church, close by Mulberry Lodge. We are hopeful that Clara and Andrew Buxton will also be able to attend, it being so near to their country home." She looked at Patience, a plea in her eyes. The response was immediate, the embrace leaving her in no doubt as to the acceptance of her request.

"Nothing you could ask of me would give me greater pleasure, Diana."

Inevitably they stopped at Hope Cottage on their way back to Worthington Place. The furniture, Gideon informed her, was to arrive the following week and they could not think of a reason why the girls should not move in with their children immediately thereafter.

"Everything inside looks so clean and just waiting for someone to make it a home. Is there much that remains to do behind the house?"

"Some fencing to ensure the animals don't wander into each other's enclosures, but little else. We are almost there, Patience, and I must admit I would like to see the ladies installed before we go to see Diana and Thomas wed. The new occupants will need as much time as they can use to get the kitchen garden planted out, for autumn will soon be upon us. Today, however, is a fine day and there are some fine walks hereabouts. What say we leave the horses tethered here, in sight of the workmen, and take a short stroll?"

She thought it an admirable suggestion and they set out at a leisurely pace, talking of the cottage and perhaps the prospect of repeating it with another in the spring, of Diana and Thomas and, though Gideon said little enough, he did confide in her that he had been worried more about Bella's future than her mother's.

"She is a delightful child and I had already put plans into place for her schooling and instruction in needlework, learning to play the piano and all those other things essential to a young lady of quality. For I am determined that she shall find her rightful place in Society, Patience. And now this will happen in the natural course of events, for Thomas will see to it, I am sure."

"So you are relieved of a burden."

"Not a burden. Never that, but certainly it is something that has bent my mind for some time. What is the matter?" he asked suddenly, alarm in his voice, for Patience had stumbled and come to a halt.

"It is nothing. I just put my foot in a hole and have twisted my ankle. Do but give me a few moments. It will be fine, I am sure."

But it wasn't, and she winced as she tried once more to put her foot to the ground. Gideon was all concern and said he would hurry back and fetch the horses and she was on no account to lower it to the ground again in the meantime. "In fact, it is fortunate that we have stopped adjacent to this gate. Allow me if you would to lift you onto the top bar, where you may sit until I return."

He put his hands on her waist and raised her as if she had been no weight at all. She came to rest on her perch, her eyes for once level with his. The birds were singing all around but between them was only silence. His hands remained where they were. Of their own volition hers rose to his shoulders. The seconds passed and no words were spoken, but an expression of anxiety on Gideon's face was gradually replaced by a warm smile, for he could see in her eyes the answer to his prayers. And then they spoke together.

"Patience, you must know…"

"Gideon, I've been such a fool."

He moved his hands now, but only for one to encircle her and the other to caress her cheek. Lips moved to meet lips and Patience knew at once that her parents' legacy had been passed to her. Gideon raised his head and said, "You have had my heart almost from the moment we met."

"And I, such a quarrelsome woman."

"It made no difference. I couldn't get you out of my mind. I thought I had no hope."

"Jasper Dysart has a lot to answer for, does he not?"

"Let this be the last time we speak of him, Patience. He played his tricks once too often and has been rumbled. He is no longer welcome in this country, and I have heard that he has escaped to France, but the truth about his character has spread across the Channel and I hear he has been exiled from polite company there too. There is no need to worry about him any more." The fleeting frown was replaced with a smile. "How very pleased my mother will be. I am certain it has for some time been her dearest wish that we marry."

"But Gideon," she said, the picture of innocence, "you have not yet asked me."

"You are right," he replied, dropping immediately to one knee. "Good heavens, what a long way up you are. Miss Worthington, will you do me the honour of becoming my wife?"

As he began to rise again, she leaned forward to speak and instead tumbled into his arms.

"And you have not yet given me an answer," he said, laughing with her, not setting her down but carrying her back towards the cottage. He placed her on the saddle and examined her foot, rubbing it tenderly. "I think it is not broken, for which I am excessively grateful. I would not have you walking on crutches on your wedding day."

"We are to be married soon then, are we?" Patience replied, loving this light banter, wondering at how quickly one's fortunes could change.

"And still I have no answer."

"Since we are being observed by no fewer than four pairs of eyes from your workmen, I must accept your kind offer or my reputation will be in shreds."

"Is that your only reason for accepting me?"

"No, Gideon, it is not. It is because I love you."

And Gideon, regardless of the observers, once more swept her off the horse and into his arms.

EPILOGUE

Worthington Place, eighteen months later

On the terrace sat six ladies. They were the Dowager Viscountess Lacey, her companion, Mary Petersham and four younger women. Nearby three children were playing with hoops on the lawn while two nurses could be seen wheeling babes in their perambulators around its perimeter.

"How delightful it is once more to be able to sit outside. It promises to be a fine summer," remarked Hester to no-one in particular.

"I believe you are right, Mama," said her daughter-in-law with a contented smile, "though I trust it will not become too oppressive, for I am already feeling the heat."

"You are increasing rapidly now, Patience, and with only two more months until your confinement it is not surprising you should be a little uncomfortable."

"I do not regard it, for I have never in my life been happier."

Clara, who was seated beside her, laughed her habitual tinkle and said, "You will not be so serene when your child is tugging at your skirts and begging to be lifted into your arms when you desire nothing so much as a few moments of solitude."

Patience was having none of it, for never was there a mother more ready to abandon everything for one of her children, who now numbered three, fate having been kind enough to bestow upon her and Andrew the daughter they had wanted for so long. Diana was quick to support Patience, saying, "Only think, Clara, what playmates Louisa and Susan will be for each other when they are a little older, for it seems to me you are spending more time at Buxton Manor than in Bath these days."

"You are right, Diana. I find since Susan was born that I am happier than I used to be when in the country, and having you and Thomas so close to hand means I always have a friend by me."

They looked across to where their nurses had stopped in the shade of some trees and were gently rocking their charges. Life had been good to them, to all of them. They had but recently welcomed into their midst Jemima Radcliff, who was now the Honourable Mrs Frederick Hildebrand, having been introduced to her husband by, of all people, the sister who he had so often tried to avoid. It was she who once again thanked Hester for hosting such a delightful house party. "This is my first since Freddie and I were married."

"It is not me you have to thank, Jemima, but my son, who enjoys nothing more than to have his friends about him. And here they come now and, if I am not mistaken, carrying rabbits, so it would seem their attempts at shooting have been successful."

As they approached, the men handed their catch to the loaders, who veered off in the direction of the servants' entrance. Their arrival was the signal for the children who had until now been playing happily on the grass to race to meet them, Bella tugging at Thomas's hand and saying, "Did you see me, Papa? Edward and William allowed me to play with them and they didn't tease me at all."

Gideon looked across at Patience, and words were not necessary between these two. Instead, he turned to Mary. She was sitting quietly, a little apart from the rest, busy with her pencils.

"Well, Mary, have you managed to capture everyone present today?"

"Merely some sketches, Gideon, but more than enough to keep me occupied for some time to come, I assure you."

Thomas put Bella on his shoulders and Andrew took each of his sons by the hand. Together they walked to where the babes were now gurgling happily on a blanket on the grass and settled down beside them, dismissing the nurses, assuring them they were quite capable of wheeling them back to the house in time for their next feed.

In the hiatus before supper Gideon joined Patience in her dressing room, where she had been reclining on the daybed for an hour.

"Are you worn out, my darling?"

"Merely obeying my doctor's orders."

"Are you sufficiently rested? I could come back later if you wish."

"I do not wish, sir, for I am now quite refreshed and eager to have a few quiet moments with you."

"Was it a mistake, do you think, to organise this party? It throws an added burden upon you."

She was quick to refute the suggestion, telling him that it was just what she needed at this time before she became so large that she could barely waddle around. This made him laugh, but he caught a fleeting look which disturbed him.

"Is something wrong?"

"Only that I am feeling gawky and don't like you seeing me this way."

He gathered her into his arms, lifted her chin and said, "Foolish girl, do you not realise you have never looked more beautiful?"

This brought tears to her eyes, so he took a few moments to reassure her. "There is one thing I do miss, though," he said, "and that is our daily rides. It has always been my favourite time of the day, and even Thunderbolt still looks for you when I take him out."

"Then I must come to the stables and reward him with an apple for his loyalty. Tell me, dearest, how goes our latest project?"

"Ready to complete in three weeks or so. I have my eye on another property which I would like you to see, but it can wait until after the baby arrives. Abigail is a gifted organiser. I am more than happy that we retained her services when you no longer required her as a companion."

"Another property? That will make six so far. Will it ever stop, do you think?"

"Not while we are needed. There will forever be unscrupulous men who are ready to take advantage of innocent young women."

"Gideon?" she said, and there was no mistaking the teasing in her voice.

He strongly distrusted her tone and said so.

"It's just that, I was wondering, with all these children, would it not be a good idea for us to build a school for them?"

"A school? Whatever will you think of next?"

"But only think. If we can give them some sort of training, they will be able to make their own way in the world and not repeat the history of their mothers. The boys can learn trades and the girls, well, I am sure there are establishments that will require their services. Anything we can teach them can only be to their benefit."

"And who do you imagine will oversee this school?"

"Why, me, of course, and Abigail. You have said yourself what a gifted organiser she is."

"I can see my predictions were correct, Patience."

"What may they have been, sir?" she said, opening her eyes wide.

"Life with you, my precious girl, will never be dull. And do you know what? I wouldn't have it any other way," Gideon said, laughing. He was still smiling as they went down to supper.

A NOTE TO THE READER

Dear Reader

I hope you have enjoyed *Love's Legacy*. If you would consider leaving a review on **Amazon** or **Goodreads**, it would be much appreciated, though I would be just as happy if you'd like to join me on my **Facebook author page** for a chat. You can also visit me on **Twitter**, **Instagram** and my **website**.

Natalie

nataliekleinman.com

Sapere Books is an exciting new publisher of brilliant fiction and popular history.

To find out more about our latest releases and our monthly bargain books visit our website:
saperebooks.com

Printed in Great Britain
by Amazon

78914488R00139